"I'm not what you expected and I suspect you don't like me very much."

He blew out a breath. "Now, where the hell did that come from?" His eyes darkened. "But you're right. You're not what I expected."

Rachel felt a twinge of disappointment. But why should he be any different from other men? And, more important, why did it matter?

"I think we should go back. It's been very— enjoyable, but all good things must…"

"You know, that's part of the problem," he said, ignoring her suggestion completely. His voice had thickened to a sensual drawl. "You're not like any woman I've known before."

"And I'm sure you've known many," Rachel retorted before she could stop herself.

"Some," he agreed, his eyes darkening again with a predatory gleam, and Rachel couldn't help herself— she started backing away. But he came after her. "Does that bother you, Ms. Claiborne? The fact that I don't want to like you, but I do?"

D0052119

All about the author...
Anne Mather

I've always wanted to write—which is not to say I've always wanted to be a professional writer. On the contrary, for years I wrote only for my own pleasure and it wasn't until my husband suggested that I ought to send one of my stories to a publisher that we put several publishers' names into a hat and pulled one out. The rest, as they say, is history. And now, more than 150 books later, I'm literally—excuse the pun—staggered by what happened.

I had written all through my infant and junior years and on into my teens, the stories changing from children's adventures to torrid Gypsy passions. My mother used to gather these up from time to time, when my bedroom became too untidy, and dispose of them. The trouble was, I never used to finish any of the stories, and *Caroline,* my first published book, was the first book I'd actually completed. I was newly married then, and my daughter was just a baby. It was quite a job juggling my household chores and scribbling away in exercise books every chance I got. Not very professional, as you can see, but that's the way it was.

I now have two grown children, a son and daughter, and two adorable grandchildren, Abigail and Ben. My email address is mystic-am@msn.com. I'd be happy to hear from any of my readers

Other titles by Anne Mather available in ebook:

Harlequin Presents®

2971–HIS FORBIDDEN PASSION
2909–THE BRAZILIAN MILLIONAIRE'S LOVE-CHILD

Anne Mather

A WILD SURRENDER

TORONTO NEW YORK LONDON
AMSTERDAM PARIS SYDNEY HAMBURG
STOCKHOLM ATHENS TOKYO MILAN MADRID
PRAGUE WARSAW BUDAPEST AUCKLAND

If you purchased this book without a cover you should be aware
that this book is stolen property. It was reported as "unsold and
destroyed" to the publisher, and neither the author nor the
publisher has received any payment for this "stripped book."

Recycling programs
for this product may
not exist in your area.

ISBN-13: 978-0-373-13069-6

A WILD SURRENDER

Originally published in the U.K. under the title *Innocent Virgin, Wild Surrender*

First North American Publication 2012

Copyright © 2010 by Anne Mather

All rights reserved. Except for use in any review, the reproduction or
utilization of this work in whole or in part in any form by any electronic,
mechanical or other means, now known or hereafter invented, including
xerography, photocopying and recording, or in any information storage
or retrieval system, is forbidden without the written permission of the
publisher, Harlequin Enterprises Limited, 225 Duncan Mill Road,
Don Mills, Ontario M3B 3K9, Canada.

This is a work of fiction. Names, characters, places and incidents are
either the product of the author's imagination or are used fictitiously, and
any resemblance to actual persons, living or dead, business establishments,
events or locales is entirely coincidental.

This edition published by arrangement with Harlequin Books S.A.

For questions and comments about the quality of this book
please contact us at Customer_eCare@Harlequin.ca.

® and TM are trademarks of the publisher. Trademarks indicated with
® are registered in the United States Patent and Trademark Office, the
Canadian Trade Marks Office and in other countries.

www.Harlequin.com

Printed in U.S.A.

A WILD SURRENDER

CHAPTER ONE

'THIS yo' first trip to St Antoine?'

Rachel dragged her eyes away from the exotic sight of hibiscus growing wild beside the airport buildings to give the taxi driver a slightly dazed look.

'What? Oh—oh, yes. It's my first visit to the Caribbean,' she admitted ruefully. 'I can hardly believe I'm here.'

And wasn't that the truth? she conceded silently. A week ago she'd had no intention of taking an unplanned break in these semi-tropical surroundings. But that had been before her father broke the news that her mother had left him. Sara Claiborne had apparently abandoned her home and her husband to fly out to the small island of St Antoine to visit a man she'd known many years ago.

'Did she say when she was coming back?'

Rachel's first thought had been a practical one, but her father had been uncharacteristically morose.

'Don't you mean *if* she's coming back?' he'd mumbled bitterly. 'And if she doesn't I don't know what I'm going to do.'

Rachel had felt out of her depth. Although she'd always believed her parents' marriage was rock-solid, occasionally she'd sensed a certain ambivalence in their treatment of each other. On top of which, her mother's attitude towards her had generally made her feel that it wasn't her problem. And if that was a little hard to take at times, she'd assumed it was simply a case of their different attitudes towards life.

Still, she had believed that Sara and Ralph Claiborne loved one another, and that, unlike lots of their friends and neighbours, their marriage was unlikely to be torn apart by rows or infidelity.

But what did she know, really? At age thirty she was still unmarried and a virgin, so any judgements she made were hardly the result of experience.

'So who is this man?' she'd asked, but her father had been carefully reticent on that point.

'His name's Matthew Brody,' had been all he'd say in response. 'He's someone she knew—years ago, as I say.' He'd paused, before exploding his next bombshell. 'I want you to go after her, Rachel. I want you to bring her home.'

Rachel had stared at him disbelievingly. 'Me?' she'd exclaimed ungrammatically. 'Why can't you go after her yourself?'

'Because I can't.' Ralph Claiborne had regarded her from beneath lowered lids. 'I just can't do it. Surely you can understand that, Rachel? What would I do if she turned me away?'

The same as me, I suppose, thought Rachel unhappily, but she could see where this was going. Whoever this man was, her father saw him as a threat to their relationship—and how could she refuse to help him when there was evidently so much at stake?

It troubled her that her mother had chosen to meet this man on an island in the Caribbean. But when she'd asked her father about this, he'd explained that Matthew Brody lived on St Antoine. It troubled her, too, that she'd never sensed the distance that must have been growing between her parents for such a potentially devastating situation to develop.

But then, she'd never been particularly close to her mother. They didn't share the same interests or like the same things. It was different with her father, but perhaps she hadn't expected as much from him.

Rachel sighed as she remembered the rest of the conversation. Her own pleas that she couldn't just walk out on her job at the local newspaper had fallen on stony ground.

'I'll have a word with Don,' said her father at once. 'I'll explain that Sara needs a break and, as I can't leave the office right now, I've asked you to take my place. He can't object to you taking a couple of weeks' unpaid holiday. Not after you've kept going when half his staff have been down with flu.'

'I've been lucky,' Rachel had protested, but it had been no use.

She knew that because Don Graham, the editor at the paper, and her father had gone to school together. Ralph Claiborne considered he was responsible for her getting a job there in the first place. And perhaps he was, although Rachel preferred not to believe it. She had been straight out of college, it was true, but with a good degree in English, and computer skills, she liked to think she'd got the job on her own merits.

Needless to say her father had been as good as his word. The following morning Don Graham had called her into his office and told her that another girl would be taking over her duties in the advertising department from now on.

'Your father says your mother hasn't been well all winter,' he'd said, and Rachel had felt her face burning. 'I'm giving you a couple of weeks' compassionate leave. Just don't make a habit of it, you hear?'

So here she was, over three thousand miles from home, without the faintest notion of how she was going to handle the situation. She was still sure her mother loved her father, but she didn't know how that love would fare in the face of another attachment. And who was this other attachment— this Matthew Brody? And why did Rachel feel such a sense of foreboding at the prospect of seeing her mother again?

'You here for a holiday?'

The taxi driver was speaking again, and Rachel knew he was only trying to be friendly. But, goodness, how could she answer that question when what she felt was that she was on the edge of a precipice with no practical means of getting down?

'Um—a holiday?' She licked her dry lips. 'Yes, I suppose so.'

It wasn't the right answer. She could see that in the dark eyes that met hers in the rearview mirror. The man's expression was both curious and wary, and she guessed he was wondering what kind of kook he was driving.

To distract herself, she turned her attention back to the view. Beyond the environs of the small inter-island airport, the road was narrow and unpaved. But the sight of the ocean creaming onto almost white sands below the thick grasses that grew on the clifftop was a definite lift to her spirits. Whatever else, she was being given a totally new—totally unexpected—experience, and she should try and get as much out of it as she could.

She'd never even heard of St Antoine before her father mentioned it to her. It was one of a small group of islands off the coast of Jamaica. Near the Caymans, but not part of them. A handful of mountains and reefs and jewel-bright vegetation where, according to her father, the only industries were a little sugar cane and coffee and, of course, tourism.

'You stayin' long?'

'Two weeks.'

At least Rachel could be honest about that. Well, providing her mother didn't send her packing the minute she saw her. That was always a possibility, and Rachel didn't know if she had a strong enough motivation to stay on under those circumstances.

Though she could, she reminded herself consideringly. Her father had booked her into St Antoine's only hotel and there was no reason why she should waste the reservation.

She'd been lucky to get it, and only because someone had cancelled at the last moment.

'You keen on water sports, miss?'

The driver was determined to learn more about her, Rachel pulled a wry face.

'I like swimming,' she admitted, not sure what else he referring to. Unless it was snorkelling. She had tried that in Spain.

'Not much else to do on St Antoine,' he persisted. 'We no movie theatres or nightclubs. Not a lot of call for stuff that.'

'I would suppose not,' murmured Rachel, a cynical s pulling down the corners of her mouth.

Well, he'd lasted a full ten minutes before making oblique reference to her appearance. She doubted the el taxi driver was interested in her, but the fact remained he already associated her with the kind of nightlife more rea found in Havana or Kingston.

She grimaced. A lifetime—an adult lifetime, anyway-parrying personal comments and sexual innuendo had ta her to ignore all references to her face and figure. So she almost six feet tall, blonde, with full breasts and long l But what of it? She didn't like the way she looked or the men looked at her. Which was probably why she was single, and likely to remain so for the foreseeable future

When she was younger, she'd used to worry about height and her appearance. She'd used to wish she was sho smaller, darker. More like her mother. Anything to a standing out in a crowd of girls her own age.

But her years at college had convinced her that boys n looked beyond the obvious. She was a blonde, therefore was a bimbo. With an IQ no bigger than her bust size.

'Is it far to town?' she asked, leaning forward, decidir take advantage of the man's garrulousness to ask some q tions of her own.

'Not far,' he replied, swinging out to pass a mule-drawn cart. It was loaded with banana plants that hung precariously over its sides. He beeped his horn and the mule jerked nervously.

'You stayin' at the Tamarisk, yeah?'

'That's right.' Rachel was grateful to discuss her destination. 'It's just a small hotel, I believe. I suppose it will be busy at this time of the year?'

'Oh, sure.' The man nodded expansively, turning the wheel of the car. The little statue of the Madonna that was suspended above his mirror swung in sympathy. 'Janu'ry, Febru'ry—they's our busiest months. 'Course, we do get visitors in summer, but when it's winter in the UK and the United States, that's when we get most tourists.' He paused. 'Like yourself.'

'Mmm.'

Rachel absorbed this, but she didn't comment. She was wondering how she could get around to mentioning Matthew Brody's name. It was a small island, and a small population. Surely it wasn't beyond the realms of possibility that he might have heard of the man?

The road that had been riding along the cliff now swung inland, and Rachel stared at the thickly wooded vegetation covering the land that rose on the right. Trees and shrubs, ferns and bushes, all exploding with colour. Even in the late afternoon, the brilliance of the sunlight was dazzling.

They were nearing the small town of St Antoine, she realised. Outlying dwellings, some of them with a plot of land given over to either cattle or crops, bordered the road, and presently an occasional store boasted signs that read 'Fresh Sandwiches' or 'Home-made Ice-cream'.

Now the road was divided into two lanes by a belt of palm trees. Rachel could see shops and houses with bougainvillea dripping from every roof and balcony. She glimpsed frangipani and oleander behind iron railings, and lots of West Indian faces peering at her as the taxi drove by.

'Um—I don't suppose you know a man called Brody?' she ventured at last, realising she couldn't afford to waste any more time. They'd be at the hotel soon and any chance would be lost.

'You mean Jacob Brody?' The taxi driver didn't wait for her to correct him before going on. 'Sure, everyone knows Jacob Brody. Seein' as how he and his son own most of the island.'

Rachel's eyes widened. Her father had told her nothing about the Brodys at all. Somehow she'd got the impression that this man—Matthew Brody—was some kind of playboy. That he and her mother must have had an affair.

'I—'

She'd been about to ask if Matthew Brody was related to Jacob when the taxi turned between wrought-iron gates. Ahead, she could see what she assumed was the Tamarisk Hotel. A two-storeyed stucco-painted structure, with a fountain playing on the forecourt out front.

'This is it.'

Her driver, a barrel-chested man, with a luxuriant moustache and cornrows, thrust open his door and got out. Then, after swinging the passenger door open for Rachel, he walked round to the rear of the vehicle to haul her suitcase out of the boot.

Rachel followed him and thrust a handful of dollars into his palm. She never knew how much to tip people, but judging by the man's expression she'd overdone it this time.

Oh, well…

'You know the Brodys?' the man asked, evidently associating her generosity with the man he'd spoken of, but Rachel shook her head.

'No,' she said, not wanting to get into a discussion. 'I can manage,' she added, when he would have carried her suitcase into the hotel. She pulled up the handle on the case to demonstrate, and then towed it after her as she walked away. 'Thank you.'

'My pleasure.' The driver stuffed the bills into his pocket. 'Yo' want anything else while you're here, yo' just let Aaron know.' He nodded towards the hotel. 'They got my number.'

Rachel doubted she'd take him up on it, but she cast him a polite smile over her shoulder. However, privately she was thinking that she'd have to be more diligent with her cash. She couldn't afford to go throwing money around, whatever happened here.

Two shallow steps that stretched along the front of the building led up to a wide verandah. Cane chairs and tables sheltered beneath the shadow of an awning, and tall columns were wound about with flowering vines. She entered into a marble-tiled foyer, where more flowers rioted from tubs and urns.

The reception desk was immediately ahead of her, but, glancing up, she saw that the second-floor rooms all opened onto a curving balcony that swept around the upper floor. The ceiling of the reception area was open to an airy atrium, and although there didn't appear to be a lift a staircase hugged the outer wall.

A pretty West Indian girl was in charge of the reception desk, and as there were few people about at the moment she watched Rachel's approach with a critical eye. Rachel doubted there was any aspect of her appearance that had gone unnoticed, but she was used to ignoring that kind of attention.

'Hi, there, welcome to the Tamarisk,' the girl said, her smile as practised as her manner. 'You have a reservation, Ms—er—'

'Claiborne,' said Rachel pleasantly. 'Yes, it was just made a few days ago.'

'Of course.'

The girl's voice had the slow, attractive drawl of the islands that Rachel had already noticed at the airport. And while she brought up Rachel's booking on the computer, Rachel took the time to examine her surroundings more fully.

The hotel was small, it was true, but it was very attractive. Not least because of the white stone pillars that supported the balcony, and the airy brightness of its public rooms. There was a pleasant scent of spices and sweetness. The air outside had been close and humid, but here the layout of the foyer allowed a cross breeze that cooled her skin.

'Here we are, Ms Claiborne.'

The girl—her name-tag read Rosa—had evidently found what she was looking for. Rescuing a pen from the drawer in front of her, she pushed a registration form towards Rachel.

'If you just fill this in,' she said, her dark eyes assessing. 'Then I'll get Toby to show you to your room.'

'Thanks.'

Rachel rested the backpack she'd carried instead of a handbag on the counter and picked up the pen. This part was familiar to her. She'd stayed in plenty of hotels before, albeit not in such exotic surroundings. She couldn't suppress a momentary twinge of excitement. Whatever else, this was an experience she wouldn't forget.

She was checking to see that she'd supplied all the necessary information when she became aware of a sudden quickening in the air. Someone else had entered the foyer, and judging by the way the receptionist straightened her spine and adjusted her cleavage it was someone she wanted to impress.

A man, then, thought Rachel cynically. She doubted Rosa would make such an effort for a member of her own sex. Unable to resist, she peeked beneath her arm and saw tan loafers and taut muscular calves clad in black denim.

Definitely a man, she conceded, straightening. Women were such clichés. Didn't they realise their reactions were so obvious to a man?

'Hi, Matt.'

Matt!

Was that a coincidence? Rachel couldn't help herself. She swung round to see who had garnered so much excitement in the building. And found herself confronted by a tall dark man, with a lean muscular frame and broad shoulders.

She supposed he was attractive in a hard athletic sort of way. She was trying to be detached about it, but for once it wasn't easy. The short-sleeved black shirt that matched his pants was coming loose from his waistband in places. So sexy. And she could see the dusky tattoo of some predatory winged beast etched around his upper arm.

He was olive-skinned and clean-shaven, although she doubted he would ever be able to erase the dark shadow on his jawline. His hair was thick and straight, and just a little too long for her liking. But he evidently ticked all the boxes so far as Rosa was concerned.

'Hey, Mr Brody's been phoning here all day, looking for you,' she said, her expression undeniably seductive. 'He's definitely on your case. I'd give him a ring, if I was you.'

'Would you, now?'

Rachel's stomach plunged. Despite being convinced now that this was the man she was looking for, his voice caused a primal leap of her senses. It was deep, dark, like black molasses soaked in treacle. Well, that was probably a contradiction, but she couldn't deny its sensual appeal.

Which bothered her quite a bit. She wasn't used to having this kind of response to a man—any man. And if this was the man her mother had apparently flown out here to meet, it was all the more disturbing.

But it couldn't be this man. Surely. He had to be at least ten years younger than Sara Claiborne and a sexy hunk besides. If he was, and her mother had succeeded in attracting his attention, she couldn't help acknowledging that Ralph Claiborne simply wasn't in his league.

She wondered what he was doing here. Was her mother

staying here, too? At this hotel? She could hardly ask him. She simply wasn't capable of making such a leap. No, somehow she was going to have to get to know this man. Would it be beyond her capabilities to gain his trust?

Her lips compressed resignedly.

Probably.

CHAPTER TWO

THE man had noticed her now.

Well, he could hardly help it, she supposed, seeing as how she was standing staring at him as if she'd never seen a man before. And because of this she felt hot colour filling her cheeks. Although she turned quickly back to the desk, she was sure he must have seen it.

Rosa was completing her reservation with one eye on what she was doing and the other on the man who was approaching the desk. She pulled open another drawer and extracted a small folder containing a key card. Then, picking up the bell beside her, she gave it a peremptory ring.

'Are you checking in?'

Rachel started. The molasses-dark voice was speaking to her now, and she swallowed convulsively before turning in his direction.

'I—oh, yes.' What it had to do with him she couldn't imagine, but she wasn't about to look a gift horse in the mouth. She licked her lips. 'Are you?'

His smile was wide, but faintly ironic, and the explanation was clear when Rosa piped up again.

'Mr Brody owns the hotel,' she said, her voice full of amused disdain. Then, as a young West Indian man appeared, she held out the key card towards him. 'Toby, will show you to your room, Ms Claiborne.' Another practised smile. 'I hope you enjoy your stay.'

'Claiborne?'

Before Rachel could move away, the man—Matt Brody—spoke. He'd come to stand beside her at the reception desk, and she was suddenly aware of the heat of his body and the clean male scent of his skin. He was taller than she was, easily six feet three or four, she estimated, and it was quite a novelty to meet a man who made her feel small.

But what was more unsettling was the fact that she was so aware of him. Of every little thing about him, actually, and that was definitely a new experience for her. A new experience, and one she didn't quite know how to handle. She'd never considered herself odd in any way because she was still a virgin at thirty. But suddenly the ramifications of her inexperience were beating a frantic path to her door.

But she wasn't here to learn about her own inadequacies, she chided herself. Or to observe his appearance—she drew the line at 'admire'—she added, as he crossed his arms over his midriff and regarded her with keen, assessing eyes. Green eyes, she saw, not dark as she'd first imagined, with long straight lashes that any woman would have died for.

'Your name's Claiborne?'

He repeated the question, and Rachel had to drag her eyes away from his fascinating tattoo to acknowledge his enquiry. 'Um—that's right,' she said. And then, with more daring than she'd given herself credit for, 'Does the name mean something to you?'

He seemed to hesitate. His dark brows drew together and the green of his irises deepened so that Rachel understood why she'd originally mistaken their colour. 'Perhaps,' he said at last. 'I have—heard of it. It's not a common name.'

'No, it's not.'

Rachel concentrated on not pursing her lips, but she was tempted to ask where he'd heard of it before. Would he be truthful? She doubted it. But she wondered what he'd say if she told him that Sara Claiborne was her mother.

'Anyway,' he added, apparently indifferent to her ambivalence, 'I hope you find your accommodation satisfactory.' He nodded towards the young man who was waiting patiently beside her suitcase. 'If there's anything else you need, just pick up the phone. I'm sure either the housekeeper or whoever's on Reception will be able to help you.'

'Thank you.'

The polite words almost stuck in her throat, but Rachel wasn't about to air her grievances in public. Despite the adrenalin that was still pumping through her veins, she couldn't deny she was weary.

It had been a long flight to Jamaica, and an unusually stressful final leg on the inter-island turboprop that had brought her from Montego Bay. The small plane had seemed to hit every air pocket over the Caribbean, and Rachel's legs had felt decidedly shaky when she'd stepped down onto the tarmac at St Antoine airport.

She would be glad to shed her clothes and take a long cool shower. And then maybe Room Service, if the hotel provided such a thing. She was enchanted by the island; she loved the individuality of the hotel. But Matt—Matthew—Brody's presence was a definite complication.

And it certainly didn't help her case to know that she was aware of him in a totally inappropriate way.

Now, forcing a thin smile, she left the reception desk to accompany the young man, Toby, across the foyer to the stairs. But she was fairly sure at least two pairs of eyes watched their progress, and she had to suppress the urge to swing her hips to show them that she didn't care.

Or was she being paranoid? And conceited? Matt Brody had given her no reason to believe he had found anything interesting about her. Only her name had struck a chord with him. And if what she suspected was true that was hardly surprising.

As she'd anticipated earlier, the rooms on the upper landing overlooked the foyer below. But inside they were light and airy, with a balcony opening off the outer wall that overlooked the gardens at the back of the hotel.

After assuring himself that she had everything she needed, Toby departed and Rachel took a few moments to explore her domain. The room wasn't large, but it was comfortable, with a large colonial-style bed, and a writing table and two armchairs.

There were chairs on the balcony, too, protected from the balcony next door by a trellis of flowering vines. Below, a kidney-shaped swimming pool dozed in the afternoon sun. The pool area was deserted at present, except for a couple of children who were playing tag around the striped umbrellas that provided shade from the blistering heat.

In other circumstances Rachel would have been enchanted. Objectively, the island was everything she could have hoped it would be. But, like all paradises, there had to be a serpent, and despite his fascination Matt Brody certainly fitted the bill.

Fascination?

Where the hell had that come from? Rachel was appalled at the way her mind had latched onto the word. Had she forgotten why she was here, or were her hormones playing tricks on her? For heaven's sake, this was not the time to find a man could be both dangerous and sexy.

The bathroom was functional, but efficient. Rachel took a long cooling shower and then dressed in the men's boxers and strappy vest she usually wore to bed. She was glad to shed the fine woollen pants and navy blazer she'd worn to travel from London; February in St Antoine was much different from February back home.

An examination of the hotel information assured her that she could order room service if she wanted. She wasn't particularly hungry—it was already midnight back in England, and normally she'd have been tucked up in bed by now—but if she didn't have something she'd be starving by the time it came to breakfast.

A green salad and ice-cream seemed innocuous enough, and while she waited she went out onto the balcony. It was dark outside, but the gardens were illuminated, casting shadows everywhere. The air was exotic, velvety-soft, and scented with a dozen unfamiliar fragrances. Rachel rested her hands on the rail and breathed deeply, trying to inhale the memory into her lungs.

She'd forgotten she was only wearing the boxer shorts and tight-fitting vest. As she raised her arms above her head her breasts moved freely beneath the cloth. She felt curiously free and elemental. The night air moved like a sensual finger against her skin.

And then she saw him. Well, she was almost sure that it was Matt Brody, standing in the shadow of one of the sunshades, his head turned upward towards her balcony.

She recoiled immediately, pulling down her hands and stepping back out of sight. Dear God, had he seen her? Well, of course he had. But what was he doing out there anyway? Surely he didn't live at the hotel.

A tap at her door had her panicking again. But then she remembered Room Service, and hastily pulled on a cotton wrapper over her vest and shorts. It was a young man she hadn't seen before, his eyes dark and admiring as they travelled over the curling dampness of her hair and the curving shape of her figure, barely concealed by the thin wrap.

'Enjoy your supper, Ms Claiborne,' he said, accepting the tip she offered with easy approval. And Rachel recognised how differently she'd reacted to two almost equally attractive men.

She ate all the salad and most of the ice-cream, nibbling on a sweetened wafer as she clambered between the sheets of the big bed. Her hair was still damp, and she supposed she ought to dry it. And she would, she told herself sleepily, as soon as she'd finished her biscuit.

It was light when Rachel awakened. She hadn't pulled the drapes the night before and the sun was streaming in through the balcony doors. At least she'd closed the door, she reflected, pushing back her hair with a lazy hand. Though the idea of anyone climbing over her balcony and invading her room was as far-fetched as her dreams.

It was only seven o'clock, but it was already far too warm in the room. She'd turned off the air-conditioning the night before, but now she pushed her legs out of bed and trudged across the carpeted floor to turn it on again. The rough shag tickled her toes, but the cool tiles in the bathroom provided a welcome contrast.

She examined her face in the mirror above the handbasin. Despite the troubling content of her dreams, she'd slept reasonably well. There were slight shadows around her eyes, and she was sure she'd acquired another wrinkle. But her skin was clear, albeit too fair for her liking, and although she'd never consider herself beautiful, her features were acceptable, she supposed.

She sighed, and, reaching for her toothbrush, started her morning routine. Nothing too complicated, just a cream cleanser to freshen her skin and a perfumed deodorant.

She still hadn't decided what she was going to do about speaking to Matt—Matthew Brody again. Or indeed how she was supposed to contact her mother. It would probably be too much to hope that she was staying at this hotel. Her father didn't have an address for her, but Rachel suspected she might be staying with the man she'd come to meet.

And where did he live?

She dressed in a short pleated skirt that left a tolerable length of leg bare and a daffodil-yellow tank top. She wore flip-flops instead of the heels she'd worn to travel in, acknowledging that if she did see Matt Brody he would seem that much taller and—maybe—intimidating.

But she didn't want to think about that. Leaving her room, she closed the door and, after glancing up and down the landing, she headed towards the stairs.

A middle-aged couple, just coming out of the room next door, said, 'Good morning'. Rachel returned their greeting with a smile, noticing how pale her skin looked beside theirs. Evidently they'd been here for several days. The man, who was fairer, was already exhibiting signs of sunburn.

At the other end of the landing a pair of double doors provided an effective barrier. As she went down the stairs Rachel wondered what was beyond them. Offices, perhaps, or a boardroom? Or the private apartment of the owner of the hotel?

Shrugging, she decided that could wait until later. She followed her neighbours down to the lobby, noticing that they knew their way around. For obvious reasons, she hadn't ventured out of her rooms again the night before.

The receptionist—not Rosa this time, but another girl—called a greeting, and Rachel had to admit that the staff were very friendly. Was it company policy, she wondered cynically, or were they just naturally gregarious people?

Like Matt Brody?

But she didn't want to go there, so instead she trailed her neighbours across the lobby and through open double doors into a casual dining area. Some of the tables were occupied inside, but most people who were there seemed to have opted for the patio. Leaving the others behind, Rachel stepped out into the sunshine with a feeling of optimism she couldn't suppress.

'Table for two?'

A waitress appeared at her elbow, and Rachel pulled a wry face. 'Just for one,' she said, half apologetically, and was unaccountably pleased when the young woman looked surprised.

She was seated at the far side of the patio. It was still early—barely eight o'clock—but the sun was already gaining in strength. She was glad of the awning that protected the tables. She didn't want to start her trip with sunstroke.

She drank freshly squeezed fruit juice and several cups of strong black coffee. Jamaica was famous for its coffee, and unless this was home-grown Rachel suspected she was enjoying a Jamaican blend. She ate only a warm roll and a Danish pastry, passing up French toast and maple pancakes, despite their delightfully appetising smell.

She was tempted to go for a swim after breakfast. Her usual routine, when she was on holiday, was to go sightseeing in the morning, before the sun became too unbearable, and then swim or sunbathe in the afternoon. But she wasn't on holiday, she reminded herself, as if any remainder was necessary. And as far as sightseeing was concerned, wasn't she more likely to find her quarry here?

She was lingering over one final cup of coffee when she became aware that someone had stopped beside her table. Someone who was tall and dark and disturbingly familiar, so that her nerves tingled and her breathing quickened, and she really had no need to look up from her abstract contemplation to find out who it was.

But of course she did.

'Good morning, Ms Claiborne.'

Matt Brody's voice caused the little hairs on the back of her neck to rise expectantly. Rachel found herself putting up a hand to calm them, half surprised to find the stubby ponytail she'd made of her hair that morning was still in place.

'Um—good morning.'

Her brief appraisal told her everything about him, and that was worrying. He, too, was wearing shorts this morning, cargo shorts that exposed brown legs and muscled calves. A white body shirt clung to every heft and sinew of his torso, once again revealing the arrow of air on his stomach.

Oh, God!

Rachel couldn't understand why she was so aware of him. Of all the men she'd ever met, and goodness knew there'd been plenty, why did she feel such a powerful reaction when Matt Brody was near?

Like mother, like daughter, perhaps?

But she refused to go there.

'Did you sleep well?'

Rachel decided she'd get a crick in her neck if she was forced to look up at him. Pushing back her chair, she got to her feet, but she still had to tilt her head to meet his gaze. Green eyes—were they mocking her?—looked mild and inoffensive. But why was he bothering with her? Had he guessed why she was here?

'Very well, thank you,' she answered, aware of the crispness of her tone. 'Did you?'

'I always sleep well, Ms Claiborne,' he said, his thin lips twitching with what could only be amusement. He paused. 'I wondered if you had any plans for this morning.'

Rachel's jaw nearly dropped. 'Plans?' she said somewhat blankly. And then, deciding he couldn't possibly know what she was thinking, she added, 'I—why, no. I was just considering my options, actually.'

Like, should I try and find out where you live, and whether my mother is staying in your house? Or if I should just wait and see what happens if you tell her that I'm here?

'Good.' He gave her a swift appraisal, and Rachel felt as if those shrewd green eyes had stripped her naked and found her wanting. 'So how do you feel about seeing a little more of the island?'

Once again Rachel felt that sense of disbelief that had accompanied his first question. 'I—yes,' she said, not at all sure what she was committing to, but prepared to take it anyway.

'I was thinking about that myself.' She took a breath. 'A[re] there guided tours?'

'You could say that.'

Matt grinned, and Rachel's stomach quivered in respons[e]. When he was relaxed, as now, he looked quite devastatin[g], his eyes crinkling at the corners, their expression softeni[ng] his masculine features.

'I was offering my services, actually,' he murmured. 'I w[as] born in England, but apart from college I've lived all my li[fe] on St Antoine. I know this place—intimately.' Had he use[d] that word deliberately? 'I guess I know places the guideboo[k] couldn't know.'

Rachel was sure he did. But she wasn't half as sure abo[ut] taking him up on his invitation. It was an ideal opportuni[ty] to question him without giving herself away. But it was al[so] far too attractive a proposition, and she wasn't at all certa[in] her father would approve.

'Um—will anyone else be coming with us?' she aske[d] innocently, and for a moment she thought his eyes darken[ed] with sudden impatience.

'No,' he said at last, his tone flat. 'Does that bother yo[u]? If I promise to keep my hands off you, will you come?'

Rachel's face flamed with colour. 'Oh, I—that is, I was[n't] implying—'

'Yes, you were.' He gave a careless shrug. 'So? What's yo[ur] answer?'

Rachel let out a nervous breath. 'Do I need to bring an[y]thing?' she asked, holding up her head, and his mouth twist[ed] consideringly.

'What did you have in mind?' he queried. And then, as [if] aware of her embarrassment, he took pity on her. 'Just som[e] sunscreen, I guess. And your swimsuit, if you have one.'

Rachel put a little space between them. 'All right,' she sa[id], mentally assuring herself that her swimsuit was the last thi[ng] she'd be putting in her bag. 'When do we leave?'

He glanced at the thick gold watch on his wrist. 'Is fifteen minutes long enough?'

Rachel nodded. 'I should think so.'

His smile was ironic. 'A woman who doesn't need the better part of an hour to get ready. How lucky am I?'

We'll see, thought Rachel, but she didn't make any comment. She was already feeling apprehensive about her decision. Regretting it, no. Fearing it, yes.

'Then I'll see you in the foyer in fifteen minutes,' he said, and with a polite nod he strode into the hotel.

Rachel had to sit down for a minute after he'd left her. She told herself it was so she could finish her coffee, but the truth was her legs felt decidedly weak.

Dear God, what had she let herself in for?

But she couldn't sit here indefinitely, she thought. She needed to go back to her room and collect the sunscreen he'd mentioned. She was determined not to take a swimsuit, though she was aware that her skirt was almost as revealing. But then when she'd packed her suitcase for the trip she hadn't expected her mother's—what? Boyfriend? Lover?—would be, at the most, ten years older than herself.

Oh, to hell with it, she chided herself impatiently. She might be a virgin, but she was still capable of taking care of herself. On her father's advice, she'd taken classes in both karate and tae-kwon-do, and although she wasn't a black belt in either, her height made her a worthy opponent.

She pulled her backpack out of the wardrobe and stowed suncream and her dark glasses inside. Then, snatching up the one-piece black swimsuit she'd bought the previous year in Barcelona, she packed that, too, adding one of the hotel's towels and daring Brody to object.

A glance in the mirror above the vanity had her pulling her hair free from the scrunchie. She usually wore it straight, but she hadn't brought her tongs with her. In consequence, it spiked up at the ends, just past her shoulders. She combed her fingers through its silky strands and decided it would have to do.

It was almost exactly fifteen minutes later when she left the room. And. to her surprise, she saw Matt Brody just coming out of the double doors at the end of the landing. So did he live in the hotel, or had he just been checking up on his house guest? she wondered. If the doors were unlocked, she might check it out herself later in the day.

A shiver of anticipation glided down her spine and she hurried down the stairs ahead of him. This was proving to be more exciting than she'd thought. She pretended she hadn't seen Matt, hoping to reach the foyer before he did. But she should have known he would be wise to a move like that.

'No hurry,' he remarked, closing the gap between them. A surprisingly callused palm closed on her bare shoulder. 'I'm right behind you.'

Rachel felt the heat of that momentary possession pass through her body like an electric current. It was only momentary, because she stumbled forward in an effort to shake him off. And almost succeeded in breaking her neck when her foot came out of one of her flip-flops. She felt herself pitching forward, her arms flailing helplessly for the rail.

But then Matt's arm slipped around her waist, dragging her back from certain disaster. Well, one disaster, anyway, Rachel taunted herself silently, feeling a hysterical desire to laugh. Being hauled up against Brody's pelvis was hardly the safest thing. She was almost sure she could feel his body stirring against her, and that offered what might be greater dangers than she'd ever anticipated.

'Th-thank you.'

Somehow she managed to extricate herself from his hold, pick up the offending flip-flop and complete the staircase on one bare foot. Then, reaching the lobby, she hastily lifted her leg and restored her footwear. In the normal way she would have bent over to accomplish the task, but the idea of giving her rescuer an uninterrupted view of her bottom was not something she wanted to pursue.

Particularly not at present.

'You okay?'

Matt came round her as she was lowering her foot to the floor again, and Rachel managed a careless nod.

'As I'll ever be, I suppose,' she declared lightly. 'It's my fault for wearing these things.' She indicated the flip-flops. 'I'd have been better off in flats.'

'You'd have been better off if you hadn't tried to outrun me,' Matt replied drily. 'What's the matter, Ms Claiborne? Do I make you nervous?'

Rachel was about to deny it, but then changed her mind. 'Perhaps a little,' she admitted tightly. 'I'm not a very tactile person, I'm afraid.'

Matt arched dark brows. 'Maybe what you mean is you're only tactile with people you like.'

'I neither like nor dislike you, Mr Brody,' she retorted, realising he was going to be more difficult than she had even imagined. She glanced towards the palm-fringed forecourt. 'Do you have a car?'

Matt regarded her silently for a long moment, and she was half afraid he was going to blow her off. She didn't want that, she realised. However reckless that made her. But, after all, this was why she'd come to St Antoine.

Then, with a casual flick of his shoulders, he gestured that she should lead the way outside. And Rachel did so, supremely aware of him following her. She should have worn her Capri pants, she thought. They would have been far more suitable. She felt totally exposed in the short cotton skirt.

CHAPTER THREE

THERE were several cars on the forecourt, some of them owned by members of the hotel staff, she assumed. Few of the guests would have their own vehicle. Unless there was a hiring franchise at the airport.

She paused, waiting for Matt to point out his car, but he passed her without a word. He headed towards the gates and she saw an open-topped Jeep parked in the street outside.

So what did that mean? she wondered. Had he just arrived at the hotel this morning? Or had the Jeep been parked there all night?

Not that he was likely to tell her. He swung open the near-side door and waited until Rachel had folded herself into the front seat. If he noticed her attempt to keep her skirt from disappearing up her thighs, she was unaware of it. But then he took her backpack from her and slung it into the back of the vehicle, apparently uncaring what might break.

'Oh, I need my sunglasses,' she objected, but Matt just ignored her and walked round to get into the driving seat.

'Try these,' he said, tossing an expensive pair of designer glasses into her lap. And, although she was sure they would be far too big for her, they fitted her face like a glove.

'Thanks.'

She glanced sideways at him as he started the engine, wondering if she dared ask him who the glasses belonged to. They were evidently not his. He'd donned a pair of Raybans as soon as he'd taken his seat, their dark lenses successfully concealing his expression.

But she said nothing, forcing herself to look about her as Matt drove away from the hotel. The small town was buzzing, even this early in the morning, with local people and tourists milling about the narrow streets.

They passed close to an open-air market, and Rachel could smell fresh fish and garlic and exotic vegetables, all mingling with the musky scents of animals and humanity. A stall selling straw hats reminded Rachel that she hadn't brought any protection. It was all right as long as the Jeep was bustling through the air, but she guessed she'd feel the heat on her head if she left the car.

However, she refused to ask Matt to stop so she could buy a hat. She would have to take care she didn't spend too long in the sun. And she probably wouldn't have the chance, she mused, judging by the speed with which Matt was driving. She had the suspicion that he was now as unenthusiastic about this outing as she was.

And that was her fault. She knew it. She had behaved quite rudely back at the hotel. It wasn't his fault that she wasn't used to being handled. He'd only saved her from a nasty fall, for heaven's sake. Not mauled her for his own ends.

The streets were quieter now. They were leaving the town behind, and now children played freely in the road, apparently indifferent to passing traffic. If Rachel had expected Matt to be impatient at having to brake every couple of minutes she couldn't have been more wrong. Instead he waved at the reckless youngsters, answering their greetings, proving how well-known and obviously well-liked he was with them.

The air was getting warmer and more humid. Rachel could see the dampness on Matt's forehead and felt a trickle of perspiration running down between her breasts. What she wasn't prepared for was Matt pulling up his shirt and using it to fan his stomach, the hair around his navel glistening with sweat.

Rachel's own stomach quivered in protest. Dear God, he was such a physical man. She discovered that, contrary to previous experiences, she wasn't immune to this man's sexuality. Quite the reverse, in fact. She wanted to reach out and touch him, to brush her fingers over that provocative growth of hair and feel the smoothness of taut brown skin.

The knowledge horrified her. As far as she knew this was the man her mother had flown over three thousand miles to see. Whatever their relationship—and she couldn't believe, having met him, that it was just friendship—her father certainly didn't expect her to get involved with him herself.

Having left the final cottages behind, they were now driving towards the ocean. Behind them, the mountains she'd seen from the taxi crowded closely towards the road. Thick vegetation turned their slopes into a lush green carpet, but ahead rough acres of uncultivated grasses descended inevitably towards the sea.

Rachel, who had been trying to remain detached about her feelings, couldn't deny a breath of wonder at the sight of blue-green water lapping a beach of pure white sand.

'It's so beautiful,' she said in a hushed voice, barely aware that they were the first words she'd spoken since they left the hotel.

Matt cast a fleeting glance in her direction, before agreeing that this was a pretty part of the island. 'Mango Cove,' he said after a moment. 'St Antoine is reputedly one of a series of peaks from an underwater mountain range. Jamaica is another.'

'Really?'

Rachel was fascinated, and Matt went on to explain that the Spaniards had first settled here at the beginning of the sixteenth century. 'Then, when Jamaica became a British colony, they ignored this island and it was later taken over by the French. San Antonio became St Antoine. End of story.'

Rachel shook her head. 'I can't understand anyone not wanting to hold on to such a beautiful place,' she protested.

'Economics, I suppose.' They'd reached a bluff above the sand dunes and Matt brought the Jeep to a halt overlooking the bay. 'Jamaica offered so much, whereas this place must have appeared to offer so little.' He pulled a wry face. 'Hey, I'm grateful. At least St Antoine isn't overrun with beach resorts and hotels.'

Rachel half turned in her seat to look at him. 'The taxi driver told me that—that the Brodys own most of the island. That would be you, right?'

Matt pulled off his dark glasses to look at her through narrowed eyes. 'Now, why would a taxi driver tell you something like that?' he asked, and for a moment Rachel didn't have an answer.

She was certainly not prepared to confront him about her mother at the moment. When—or even if—she did so, she would hope it was in a place less isolated than this. But at the same time she had to say something. Even if he must suspect her motives just as much as she suspected his.

'I—er—I was asking him about the plots of land around the houses. I said I thought they were cute, but he said the tenants didn't own them. That—that the Brodys did.'

'Really?' Matt looked sceptical. 'Well, for your information, the island people *do* own their own plots of land.' He gave her one final speculative glance and then thrust open his door. 'We encourage people to be self-sufficient.' His lips twisted. 'Your taxi driver got it wrong.'

'So it would seem.' Rachel kept a wary eye on him as he got out of the Jeep. Then, pushing open her own door, she did likewise, feeling the heat of the sun on her arms and the delicious breeze off the water.

Matt pushed his glasses back onto his nose and went ahead

of her. Slipping and sliding, he descended the dunes to arrive unscathed at the beach.

He turned then. 'You coming?' he asked, and Rachel decided she didn't have much choice. Besides, she wanted to paddle in the water. Her feet were already itching to feel the sand between her toes.

Hauling her backpack out of the back of the Jeep, she removed the flip-flops and then followed him. It wasn't as easy going down the dunes as he'd made it look, and she arrived at the bottom dishevelled and red-faced.

Thankfully, Matt had already walked away towards the water. And, putting down her pack, she combed her fingers through her hair again, realising that trying to look neat at the moment was far beyond her capabilities.

Shouldering the pack again, she started after him, and then paused for a second to examine a huge pink shell that was honeycombed with cracks. Evidently something had lived inside it once, but its sanctuary had been invaded. Or perhaps it was very old and had been eroded by the sea.

The sun was beginning to beat down on her head now, as well as on her shoulders. When she straightened, she lifted a hand to protect her scalp.

'You hot now?'

Her interest in the shell had not gone unnoticed, and Matt had made his way back to her. Like her, he'd shed the Converse trainers he'd been wearing, tying the laces together and hanging them round his neck.

'A bit,' Rachel admitted, and Matt nodded towards the sea.

'Take a dip,' he advised. 'That will cool you down. You might even enjoy it.'

Rachel pursed her lips. 'How do you know I've brought a swimsuit?'

Matt pulled off his glasses again, his eyes mocking and

intent. 'Hey, I'm not a prude,' he said. 'We can go skinny-dipping, if you like. I'm game if you are.'

Why did he always have the power to embarrass her? As her face flamed with colour, Rachel hoped it would just blend in with the flush that already stained her cheeks.

'I know you're not serious,' she said primly, although she was half afraid he was. 'But I have brought a swimsuit, as it happens. If you'll look the other way, I'll put it on.'

Matt's mouth showed his amusement. 'Now who's a prude?' he asked. 'I can't believe you've never undressed in front of a man before.'

As a matter of fact she hadn't, but Rachel wasn't about to tell him that. 'Just turn the other way,' she said tersely. 'I'm not about to undress in front of a man I barely know.'

'Your loss.'

But to her relief he did turn his back and saunter away towards the ocean. Though her deliverance was tempered with disbelief when he hauled his shirt over his head and flung it down on the sand. Then his hands went to the waistband of his shorts.

Rachel's mouth fell open and she paused in the middle of unbuttoning her skirt. What on earth was he doing? she wondered. And then let out a gasp when he dropped his shorts as well.

He was wearing underwear.

Rachel relaxed a little when she saw black shorts. She'd been half afraid he went commando. But, dear God, what would her mother think? she mused, dumbfounded. Did she know he flirted with other women when she wasn't around?

And yet he hadn't actually flirted with her, she conceded honestly, stripping off her skirt and panties, pulling her swimsuit over her hips. It wasn't his fault that she reacted to him. He was just naturally unconventional, naturally uninhibited, the kind of man Rachel had never had dealings with before.

Her tank top and bra were quickly disposed of, and she

expelled another sigh when the top of the swimsuit was se
curely in place. Okay, it was strapless, and probably not th
most appropriate choice in these circumstances. But she'
change back into her clothes as soon as she'd had a swim.

Matt was already in the water, the sea lapping about hi
hips. His tattoo was fully exposed now, wrapped darkl
around his upper arm. She noticed how brown his skin wa
above his black waistband, smooth and unblemished. He ha
narrow hips and strong thighs and a tight muscled butt.

Dear Lord, she wasn't supposed to notice such things, no
about a man who was apparently involved with her mother
But, for some reason she preferred not to dwell on, she wa
incapable of ignoring him, or his hard masculine beauty.

Choosing a spot some yards from where Matt had entere
the water, Rachel dragged her eyes away from her tormento
and ran eagerly into the sea. It was so good to submerge he
shoulders, to dip her head below the surface, to come up feel
ing exhilarated just to be alive.

The land shelved fairly steeply, she discovered, and in n
time at all she was out of her depth. But that didn't worry he
She was a strong swimmer, and the water itself was so warn
and soft and delightful. Whatever else she took from this tri;
she would always remember swimming in the Caribbean.

She'd been half afraid that as soon as she was in the wate
Matt would join her. Or was that half hopeful? she wondered
aware of something like disappointment when he kept away
He was some distance further out, turned onto his back an
floating on the water. A dark star-shaped figure that attracte
her like a magnet.

She couldn't help herself. She swam towards him and sai
breathlessly, 'Isn't it marvellous? I've never swum in wate
as clear as this.' She'd already noticed dozens of tiny fisl
swimming beneath her. 'Thank you for bringing me here.'

'No problem.'

With knife-like grace, Matt brought his legs up to his bod

and then straightened to tread water beside her. He'd left his dark glasses on the beach, as she had, and his eyes were unmistakably sardonic.

'I got the impression you wished you hadn't accepted my invitation,' he said, reaching out to wipe a strand of wet hair from her face. He saw her flinch and his expression hardened. 'Lighten up, can't you? Or do you think every man who touches you wants to jump your bones?'

'I'm sure you don't, Mr Brody,' she retorted, her enjoyment of the day souring on the bitterness of his words. Without waiting for his response, she turned and swam back towards the shore. He was impossible, she thought irritably. He turned everything into a personal assault.

Matt overtook her before she reached the shallows, so she was obliged to follow him as he walked up out of the water. But she found her stomach tightening instinctively when she got a good look at his underwear. He was wearing black stretch boxers that clung to him like a second skin.

He turned, picking up his body shirt and using it to dry his chest and stomach. As before, he didn't seem to care what she thought of his behaviour, but Rachel was finding it very hard to drag her eyes away. It infuriated her, but she found everything about him unbearably sexy. She was beginning to understand why the girls in the office gossiped constantly about their sexual experiences.

The bravado of bringing one of the hotel towels seemed unnecessary now. Rachel felt distinctly guilty when she pulled the towel out of her backpack. But Matt wasn't looking at her. As he continued to rub his chest and arms, his attention seemed fixed on a large bird foraging among debris further along the sand.

Rachel couldn't help herself. Wrapping the towel about her, she exclaimed, 'What is that?'

'A pelican.' Matt sounded indifferent. 'It's evidently found

something to eat amongst the seaweed. This beach is usual
deserted. I guess it thought it wouldn't be disturbed.'

'A pelican.' Rachel shook her head in wonder. 'I've nev
seen a pelican before.' She looked at Matt. 'Is that what you'
got tattooed on your arm?'

'Hell, no.' Matt shook his head, though his gaze barel
acknowledged her. 'This is a nighthawk. I had it done whi
I was at college. My father didn't approve, but it was too la
then to do anything about it.' He grimaced. 'Finish gettin
dressed. Then I'll take you back to the hotel.'

'Oh.' Rachel let out a sigh. 'Must we?'

Matt's frown wasn't encouraging. 'Must we what?'

'Go back,' Rachel said, knowing he'd understood her th
first time. 'Look, I know I overreacted before, but that's ju
me.'

'Really?'

His frown deepened, but he didn't immediately say any
thing else. Instead, to her amazement, he turned his back o
her and pushed his wet boxers down his legs.

Rachel's eyes widened. She'd been right. He was totall
uninhibited. He didn't care who saw him, or that she migl
find his behaviour offensive.

But she couldn't deny he was good to look at. Wide shou
ders tapered to narrow hips, his buttocks rounded and tigh
And he was brown all over. No boring privacy line for hin
As he used his shirt to dry himself again, Rachel found sh
was holding her breath.

She didn't suck another gulp of air into her labouring lung
until he'd pulled on his cargo shorts. He wrung out the boxer
he'd worn to swim in, and then put on the damp body shir
that clung even closer now. She could count the vertebrae i
his spine, the neat lacing of muscles over his stomach. An
then she realised, with a sense of frustration, that she hadn
even begun to get dressed herself.

Fool, she thought impatiently. She was acting like a moor

struck schoolgirl. Heaven knew what her mother would think if she could see her now.

She fumbled beneath the towel, trying to dislodge the swimsuit. But her body was wet, the suit damp and clingy. She couldn't help thinking how much easier it would be if she dared drop the towel and strip in front of him.

Of course she didn't do any such thing. And to her relief Matt bent to gather up his shoes. With a supreme effort she managed to kick the swimsuit off her legs. It was fairly simple, after that, to step into her skirt and panties using the towel to protect her as she pulled on her tank top.

It was only as she was stuffing the damp towel into her backpack that she saw her bra still lying on the sand. She said a rude word under her breath, but it was too late to worry about it now. She stuffed it into the bag, too, suddenly aware that Matt had started away along the shoreline.

He glanced back when she straightened, however, and his timing was so perfect she had to wonder if he'd been as indifferent to her struggles as she'd believed.

'Let's walk,' he said neutrally, apparently prepared to humour her. 'If you can stand the heat.'

'I think I can.'

Rachel slung the backpack over her shoulder and hurried to catch up with him. But when she came level he reached over and lifted the bag from her arm.

'Leave it here,' he said, dropping it onto the sand. He spread an all-encompassing arm. 'No one's likely to steal it.' He pulled a wry face. 'Except him, of course.' He indicated the pelican, who looked poised for flight. 'But I doubt he'd find one of my towels to his taste.'

Rachel glanced up at him. 'I know. I shouldn't have brought it.'

'Did I say that?'

'You didn't have to. I feel guilty enough as it is.'

'Forget it.' He dismissed her claim. 'What's one towel or more between enemies?'

Rachel caught her breath. 'Are we enemies, Mr Brody?'

'Matt,' he corrected her shortly. And then, 'Well, we're sure as hell not friends.' He started to walk again. 'Come on. Keep moving. Or you're going to need to cover up.'

Which wasn't his problem, thought Rachel, trying to distract herself. But if she wanted to stay with him she had to do as he said. And it was surprisingly pleasant, walking in the shallows, feeling the sand melting away between her toes.

They walked for a while in silence. Rachel had expected to feel uncomfortable after what he'd just said, but she didn't. In actual fact she enjoyed the sense of isolation, with only the cry of birds and the muted thunder of the ocean to disturb the peace.

And then he asked the question she'd been dreading.

'Why did you come to St Antoine, Ms Claiborne?'

CHAPTER FOUR

Matt had halted and Rachel was forced to do the same.

She took a breath. 'My name's Rachel, as I'm sure you know.'

'Okay.' He was tolerant. 'Why did you come to St Antoine, *Rachel*?'

She couldn't tell him. Not like this. Not so baldly. She just couldn't.

'Um—why do people usually come to the island?' she prevaricated lightly. 'I needed a break and St Antoine seemed an ideal place to chill.'

'To chill?'

Sceptical eyes drifted down over the defensive angle of her jaw to the creamy hollow of her throat.

And beyond.

Rachel was instantly aware of the disadvantages of not wearing a bra when his eyes lingered on her cleavage. The hard peaks of her breasts must be clearly visible, taut against the soft fabric of her top. And, short of covering them with her hands, there was nothing she could do about it.

'You should have gone to the South Pole,' he remarked mockingly. 'I'm told it's pretty chilly there.'

Rachel's nostrils flared. 'I think you know what I meant.'

'Yeah.'

He conceded the point and started walking again. And

Rachel was so relieved to be free of those scathing eyes s[..]
fell into step beside him.

But he wasn't finished.

'That doesn't really explain why you chose this island,'[..]
persisted. 'I mean, we're not exactly on the tourist map.'

'You get tourists here.'

'They're often recommendations,' Matt informed h[..]
smoothly. 'And usually from the States.'

Rachel managed a short laugh. 'You know, if I didn't kn[..]
better, I'd think that you didn't welcome new visitors, [M]
Brody. If all your guests are subjected to this inquisition.'

'Matt.' He stopped again, his voice hardening with imp[..]
tience. 'And they're not.'

'Oh.' Rachel made a moue of her lips. 'Well, I'm here no[..]
She paused. 'I'm sorry if I'm in the way.'

Matt studied her apparently innocent expression for anot[..]
long disturbing moment, and then made a chopping moveme[..]
with his hand.

'Did I say you were in the way?' he demanded. 'You [..]
intrigue me, that's all. Put it down to simple curiosity, if y[..]
like, but I don't think you're being entirely honest about y[..]
reasons for being here.'

What did he know?

Rachel sucked in a breath. 'Are you calling me a liar, [M]
Brody?'

'Don't put words in my mouth, Ms Claiborne. There's [..]
expression I've heard that seems relevant. I think you're bei[..]
economical with the truth.'

Rachel turned away and started walking again. She co[..]
feel his eyes boring into the back of her head, but she forc[..]
herself to put one foot in front of the other.

'I must say, you don't pull your punches, Mr Brody,' s[..]
threw back over her shoulder. 'And here was I, thinking yo[..]
enjoyed my company.'

'Whether or not I enjoy your company has nothing to [..]

with it,' he retorted, overtaking her. He stepped in front of her. 'And for God's sake stop calling me *Mr* Brody.'

Rachel made an effort to appear composed. But it was difficult with approximately two hundred pounds of frustrated male more or less in her face.

'All right. *Matt*,' she said with assumed lightness. 'You don't have to humour me. I'm not what you expected and I suspect you don't like me very much.'

He blew out a breath. 'Now, where the hell did that come from?' His eyes darkened. 'But you're right. You're not what I expected.'

Rachel felt a twinge of disappointment. But why should he be any different from other men? And, more importantly, why did it matter? He was her mother's problem, not hers.

'I think we should go back,' she said, concentrating on the unbuttoned neckline of his body shirt. Which wasn't the most sensible place to look, bearing in mind the dark hair that was clearly visible in the opening. But at least it kept her gaze away from his. 'It's been very—enjoyable, but all good things must—'

'You know, that's part of the problem,' he said, ignoring her suggestion completely. His voice had thickened to a sensual drawl. 'You're not like any woman I've known before.'

'And I'm sure you've known many,' Rachel retorted before she could stop herself. But, heavens, what was she supposed to say?

'Some,' he agreed, his eyes darkening with a predatory gleam, and Rachel couldn't help herself. She started backing away. But he came after her. 'Does that bother you, Ms Claiborne? The fact that I don't want to like you but I do?'

Rachel's jaw dropped. 'Are you coming on to me, Mr— *Matt*? Because I think I should warn you, I do know how to defend myself.'

'Oh, for heaven's sake!' With a muffled oath, Matt strode past her. 'Listen to yourself, will you?' His long legs opened a yawning space between them. 'Get your rucksack. We're going back.'

'It's a backpack,' muttered Rachel barely audibly as she hurried after him.

They'd walked a surprisingly long way, and she had to jog back to where her bag was lying before practically running to reach the place where they'd left the Jeep.

She was still muttering to herself as she struggled to climb the dunes, getting frustrated when the sand persisted in sliding away beneath her feet. She'd watched Matt navigate them without any apparent effort, and it was infuriating to see him standing at the top, watching her make an absolute idiot of herself.

'You might have helped me,' she panted when she got to the top, but Matt only lifted both hands, palms towards her.

'What? And be accused of taking advantage of one of my guests?' he mocked. 'And besides, why should I deprive myself of such an amusing exhibition?'

Rachel's lips pursed. 'Moron!'

Matt shrugged. 'Bimbo!'

Rachel gasped. 'I'm not a bimbo!'

'And I'm not a moron, Ms Claiborne. I suggest you get in the vehicle and I'll take you back to the hotel.'

Rachel wrenched open the door of the Jeep and did as he suggested. For his part, Matt pulled what she saw were the damp pair of boxers out of his pocket and tossed them into the back of the car. Then he climbed in beside her, the waistband of his shorts dipping revealingly at the back, reminding her, if any reminder was necessary, that he was naked under them.

They seemed to get back to the hotel far more quickly than Rachel had expected. In no time at all, Matt was drawing up outside the Tamarisk's gates.

Rachel thrust open her door and jumped out, turning to make some perfunctory offer of thanks. But Matt just said,

'Enjoy your day,' and drove away without giving her time to speak.

Rachel's mouth compressed frustratedly, but there was nothing she could do. He'd gone, and with him any chance of asking him about her mother. Although whether she'd have actually had the nerve to do that was anyone's guess.

Reaching her room, she found the message light on her phone was flashing. Lifting the receiver, she connected with Reception and then said, 'I believe you have a message for me.'

As she waited for the girl to reply, it crossed her mind that it could be her mother. If Matt had mentioned her arrival to her, she might have decided to get in touch.

'Ms Claiborne?'

The girl was speaking again, and Rachel answered in the positive. 'I'm here.'

'I have here a note that says your father called at nine o'clock this morning,' the receptionist intoned leisurely. 'He asked if you'd ring him as soon as you came in.'

Of course. It had to be her father, thought Rachel grumpily. He'd probably expected her to phone him last night, although bearing in mind the time change that had surely not been on the cards.

'Okay. Thank you,' she said now, and put down the receiver. She needed a few moments to compose what she was going to say before she made the call.

Eventually, though, she dialled for an outside line and punched in the numbers of her parents' home. For years they'd all lived in a comfortable house in Chingford, but when Rachel had moved into an apartment of her own her parents had sold the house and bought an apartment themselves.

'Hello?'

Her father's voice was surprisingly welcome. Despite the argument they'd had about her coming here, he was still her best friend in the entire world. She loved her mother. There was no doubt about that. But the aloofness she'd always detected in her mother's attitude towards her had made any real closeness between them difficult.

'Hey, Dad.' Rachel tried to sound upbeat. 'Sorry I was out when you called.'

'Where were you?'

Instead of making some reassuring comment, Ralph Claiborne was immediately on the offensive.

'I—I took a tour of the island,' Rachel finally replied, a little defensively. 'I was going to ring you as soon as I got back.'

'Hmmph!' Her father didn't sound mollified. 'So, what's happening? Have you spoken to your mother yet?'

'Are you kidding?' Rachel was indignant. 'We're not talking Camberwick Green here, Dad. This may be a fairly small island, but I should think its population runs into tens of thousands.'

'Does it?'

'Yes.' Rachel sighed. 'You're going to have to give me some leeway, Dad. I can't be making a report to you every single day.'

'No one's asking you to phone every single day,' he shot back, evidently on edge. 'Just keep me in the loop, Rachel. That's all I ask.'

'And I will. When I have something pertinent to tell you.' Rachel crossed her fingers, aware that she wasn't being honest with him either. 'Anyway, how are you? How are you managing on your own?'

'Oh, I'm all right.' He was dismissive. 'Your aunt Laura brought me a cooked meal last night.' He snorted. 'The damn woman can't keep away.'

'Well, you watch what you're doing,' said Rachel reprovingly. 'You know Aunt Laura's always had a soft spot for you. I'd hate you to get involved with her when Mum's probably going to be home in a couple of days.'

'You think?'

He didn't sound optimistic, and, knowing all the facts, Rachel couldn't blame him. If her mother was involved with Matt Brody, she was unlikely to want to give him up any time soon.

'Leave it to me,' she said firmly, with more confidence than circumstances allowed. 'I'll give you a ring in a couple of days, unless you hear something before I do.'

'As if I'm going to.' Her father sounded depressed now. 'Thank God I didn't retire last year as your mother wanted.'

Ralph Claiborne was an accountant, working for a small firm in Charing Cross. But now Rachel had to wonder if his refusal to retire might have been the trigger that had set the present events in motion. Maybe her mother was lonely. Still, that wasn't really an excuse for what she'd done.

'Okay, Dad,' Rachel said now. 'I'm going to go and take a shower and then have some lunch. This is a super hotel.' Owned by the Brodys. But that was something she couldn't discuss right now. 'I'm glad you chose it.'

'Well, I'm glad I've done something right, then,' said her father shortly. 'But you're not there to enjoy an unscheduled holiday, Rachel. You know what I expect you to do. Find your mother.'

'Yes, Dad.'

Rachel winced at the pain in his voice, and long after she'd replaced the receiver she sat there just staring at the phone. But without Matt Brody's help she hadn't the first idea of how she was going to find Sara Claiborne. This was the only hotel on the island, according to the taxi driver, and surely the receptionist would have made the connection if her mother was staying here.

During the next couple of days Rachel made a concerted effort to find out everything she could about alternative accommodation on the island. She found an information booth in town, and was able to get the names of several B and Bs from them. She checked them out without any luck, but she wasn't totally surprised. And there was no way she could mention her search to the receptionist at the Tamarisk without arousing more questions than answers.

On the third day she made her way down to the harbour. Despite her investigations, for the first two days she'd suffered from jet-lag and had needed to rest in the afternoons. She had gone down to the pool for a swim in the early evening, however—the water was deliciously warm then, and mostly deserted—before returning to her room to dress for dinner.

She was falling into quite a routine, and she knew she had to put a stop to it. It was far too easy to relax here, even if the sight of Matt Brody still caused goosebumps to feather her spine. She'd seen him once or twice, going in and out of the hotel, but there'd never been a confrontation. Whether that was his fault or hers, she couldn't be certain. But she was fairly sure he was avoiding her.

Which wasn't helping her father's cause at all. She knew he'd feel so betrayed if he learned she'd spoken to Matt Brody without even mentioning her mother's name.

But how could she? Rachel asked herself. She'd only spent a couple of hours in Matt's company, when all was said and done. They weren't even friends. They were more like enemies now. How could she have asked him such a personal question? *Are you having an affair with my mother?*

The harbour was as pretty as the rest of the island. Several fishing boats were anchored on one side of a small stone pier, with a surprisingly busy marina occupying the other. A number of yachts with reefed sails bobbed in the current, their distinctive mooring bells carrying musically on the breeze.

There were motor yachts, too. Huge expensive things, with tiered decks and gleaming brass furniture. One of them even had a small pool, but it was empty at present. Its owner was probably enjoying the freedom of moving from place to place.

Rachel leaned on the rail overlooking the marina. She was wearing shorts this morning, and a blue silk vest she'd bought in the hotel shop. She was admiring her slight tan when she saw a big man emerge from one of the slips. He was formally attired, in pleated khakis and a dress shirt, open at the neck. He was wearing a tie, too, pulled away from his collar. His dark hair was ruffled by the breeze, but there was no mistaking that it was Matt Brody, real and in the flesh.

Her instincts were telling her to walk away, now, before he looked up and saw her. All right, she wasn't doing anything wrong, but would he believe her being here was purely a coincidence? She remembered he'd avoided her at the hotel. Or at least made no effort to speak to her again. And after her behaviour at the beach she couldn't exactly blame him.

She guessed he'd come from one of the motor vessels. The yacht behind him wasn't the biggest in the marina, but it wasn't the smallest either. He wasn't dressed for sailing, so what was he doing here?

Despite her misgivings, she knew she ought to make an effort and speak to him. For her father's sake, if nothing else. How was she ever going to find out where her mother was if she didn't open the lines of communication, as they said in the best spy dramas? Where was the harm? If he blew her off, she could at least say she'd tried.

Rachel took a breath, preparing to call a greeting, when she saw a young woman emerge from the yacht behind him. The sound she'd been about to make was stifled in her throat. Evidently they were together. The girl was hurrying, trying to catch him up.

'Wait,' she called, her voice showing her agitation. 'Matt, wait for me. D'you want me to break my heel on these damn boards?'

She was a beautiful young woman, Rachel noticed. Not

particularly tall, but slender and graceful, with short black hair and elfin features. But right now her mouth was drawn down in a scowl, her ill humour evidently directed towards her companion.

'I didn't ask you to come here,' Matt called back over his shoulder, his voice carrying clearly over the water. And Rachel felt like a voyeur, no matter how innocent her eavesdropping might be.

'I know that,' the girl huffed as she caught up with him. She grabbed his arm familiarly and he didn't shake her off. 'But I wanted to speak to you privately and you're never around.'

Matt helped her negotiate the gate that led out of the mooring area. 'What you mean is, you don't usually get up before midday.'

'I need my sleep,' she protested, as they disappeared under the overhang of the jetty.

And Rachel realised they were probably heading for the stone stairs that she could see just a few yards away along the pier.

Once again, the urge to escape before they saw her was compelling. Whoever the girl was, Matt was evidently familiar with her sleeping habits. Which begged the question, how many women was he involved with?

However, before she could decide what she wanted to do, Matt appeared at the top of the steps. He stretched out a hand to help the young woman up beside him, and then they both started walking towards the quay. Towards Rachel.

Matt recognised her at once. Rachel thought he cast a brief glance down at his companion, but he didn't slow his stride. Whoever she was, he wasn't concerned that Rachel had seen her with him, and as before it was left to the girl to keep up with him.

'Hi.' As soon as they were within speaking distance, Rachel spoke. She was conscious that her greeting had caught the other girl unawares. 'It's a lovely morning, isn't it?'

'They're all lovely mornings on St Antoine,' replied Matt tersely, and she was sure his intention had been to walk right by her.

But the girl caught his arm again, and he came to an evidently reluctant halt. 'Except in the hurricane season,' she said, narrowing her eyes at Rachel and assessing her appearance with an intensity that was far from objective. 'Are you staying on the island? Ms—er—?'

'Rachel,' Rachel supplied a little stiffly. She knew Matt was looking at her with unconcealed impatience. Clearly he hadn't wanted to do more than acknowledge her, and then only because she'd spoken first. 'I'm staying at the Tamarisk.'

'Oh. You're staying at the hotel.' The girl raised dark brows and glanced up at the man beside her. 'How interesting.' She paused. 'Isn't it, Matt?'

Matt's response was merely to shrug his shoulders, and the girl absorbed this before turning back to Rachel to ask enquiringly. 'Are you staying long?'

Rachel objected to these questions. Particularly from someone she hadn't even been introduced to. But if she wanted to retain Matt's attention she had to be polite.

'Uh—no,' she said now. 'Just a couple of weeks, actually. I don't think the hurricane season will bother me.'

'Or Amalie either.' As if he felt compelled to make some contribution to the conversation, Matt released himself from the girl's fingers and gave Rachel an appraising look. She was instantly conscious of the limitations of narrow-legged shorts and trainers, but Matt's eyes were coolly uninterested. 'When the hurricane season comes around my sister's usually tucked up safely in New York.'

She was his sister!

Rachel's tongue ran nervously over her upper lip. It shouldn't have been such a relief to her, but it was. 'So,' she ventured, 'have you been sailing?'

'In this outfit?'

Amalie rolled her eyes, and Rachel felt foolish for having suggested such a thing.

'I was just checking out the boat,' Matt put in, apparently taking pity on her. 'We've got a group of fishermen coming in tomorrow, and they plan on taking it up to Grand Cayman.'

'Oh...' Rachel nodded. 'It's a charter.'

'Yeah, a charter.' Amalie chimed in again. 'My brother insists on checking the boats out himself.'

Rachel's eyes widened. 'You've got more than one?'

'Heavens, yes. We've got—'

'—more than one,' Matt broke in before Amalie could finish. 'And now, if you'll excuse us...'

'Actually...' Rachel wasn't accustomed to soliciting a man's company, but she had to try. 'I was wondering if you—and your sister, of course—might like to join me for a—a coffee or something.'

The girl was the first to speak. She gave Rachel a measuring look and then gazed up at Matt, her expression frankly mocking. 'Hey, I think you're being propositioned, darling,' she said musingly. 'Methinks the lady wants to get in your pants!'

CHAPTER FIVE

'For God's sake, Amalie!'

Matt swore, evidently infuriated by her comment, but Rachel was sure he couldn't possibly feel as bad as she did at that moment. Without knowing anything about their history— or at least Rachel didn't think she did—Amalie had assumed she was coming on to her brother.

'What? *What?*'

Amalie feigned innocence, but Rachel was sure she'd known exactly how her brother would react.

'Grow up!' said Matt harshly. 'Not all women think about sex every minute of the day. Don't judge everyone by your standards, Amalie. Keep your sordid comments to yourself.'

'All right, all right.' Amalie looked sulky now, and she lifted her hands defensively. Then she turned to Rachel. 'You weren't offended, were you?'

Rachel mumbled something non-committal, but that didn't stop Amalie from continuing. 'I mean, we're both women of the world, aren't we? And, as you're probably a little older than me, yeah, I bet you've—known quite a few exciting men in your time.'

The pause before the word 'known' wasn't lost on Rachel. She wondered what Amalie would say if she told her she was still a virgin. She probably wouldn't believe her. Most people didn't. Particularly men.

'Whether or not Rachel was offended, I was,' stated Matt

harshly. 'Take the Jeep and go back to the house, Amalie. I'
get Caleb to come and get me when I'm through.'

'Oh, but Rachel asked me to join you for a cup of coffee
Amalie objected.

'Rachel didn't know you had to leave.' Matt's tone wa
unyielding. 'D'you want to argue with me?'

'No,' Amalie said broodingly. 'You know, you're no fun
would have liked a cup of coffee, as it goes.'

'Get one back at the house,' Matt advised her tersely. An
looking at his expression, Rachel didn't think she would ha
argued with him either.

'But we never got to talk.' Amalie gazed up at him appea
ingly.

'Okay.' Matt didn't sound particularly amenable. 'Ho
about if I promise we'll talk tonight?'

'Tonight?' Amalie wailed.

'Yeah. Be at home for dinner. We'll have plenty of time
discuss your financial problems then.'

Amalie pursed her lips. 'But what about Tony?'

'Tony Scabo?'

'Yes. I said I'd see him tonight.'

'Well, bring him to dinner. I'm sure he'll be interested
hear what you have to say.'

'Beast!' Amalie pouted. Then her eyes flickered Rachel
way. 'Just don't think I'm a fool,' she snapped shortly, ar
with another loaded glance in Rachel's direction she teetere
away on her ridiculous heels.

'I'm sorry if I caused a problem,' Rachel murmured whe
his sister was out of earshot.

'Are you?' Matt didn't sound as if he believed her. 'Isr
that your role here, causing me problems?'

'I don't know what you mean.'

'No? So why are you suddenly being so friendly? The la
time we were together you told me I was a moron.'

Rachel's face flamed. 'You called me a bimbo!'

'Only in self-defence.'

'Well, anyway, I was wrong. You're not a moron. I'm sorry if I was rude. Now, can we just bury our differences and move on?'

'Why?'

'Why?' She was taken aback by the question.

'Yeah. Why should you care what I think?'

'Well…' Rachel's tongue circled her lower lip this time. 'Let's just say I do.' She paused. 'Will you have coffee with me?'

'Are you coming on to me, Ms Claiborne?'

'Oh, for heaven's sake!' Rachel knew he was just being sarcastic, but that didn't alter her frustration. 'You really are the most infuriating man I've ever known.'

'And you've known quite a few—is that what you're saying? Amalie seemed to think you knew your way around.'

'Amalie was wrong,' said Rachel crossly. 'Don't let my appearance fool you, Mr Brody.'

'You mean because you have the kind of face and figure that might make a man think of sex?'

'No.' Rachel knew he was only baiting her, but she had to make some defence. 'I just wanted you to know that I don't spend my time jumping in and out of other people's beds.'

'I assume you mean *men's* beds,' Matt murmured, a hint of laughter in his voice, and she sighed.

'Can we just leave it?' she demanded. 'Do you want to join me for coffee or not?'

'Do I still have a choice?'

'Of course.'

Matt shrugged. 'Why not? If you'll promise to stop calling me *Mr* Brody.' They began to stroll back towards the quay. 'So—are you enjoying your holiday? You're not finding it lonely, being on your own?'

'Is that why you think I've asked you to have coffee with me?' she countered immediately, and Matt gave her a resigned look.

'Uh, no,' he said mildly. 'Believe it or not, it was a perfectly innocent question. But if you don't want to answer it, hey, that's all right with me.'

Rachel pressed her lips together. Somehow he always managed to make her feel small. 'As a matter of fact, I haven't had time to feel lonely. I've been exploring the town, getting over jet-lag.' She grimaced. 'It was only when I saw you that I thought I ought to take the chance to make amends for the way I behaved that first day.'

Matt cast a sideways glance at her. 'You weren't curious about Amalie's identity?'

Rachel looked away so he wouldn't see the sudden blush that filled her cheeks. 'Why should I be?' she asked. Then, 'Will you decide where we should go for coffee? Is there somewhere special that only the locals know?'

Matt said nothing for a moment, and then he gestured across the harbour road to a small café set up off the street. Rachel might never have noticed it if he hadn't pointed it out. It looked more like a night spot with its outdoor bar and seating area.

'Juno's,' he said. 'She's a good friend of mine. And she just happens to serve the best coffee in St Antoine.'

'Okay.'

Rachel was grateful for the need to dodge the traffic to give her time to compose herself again. Walking quickly, she managed to keep up with his long strides, and they crossed the sidewalk and climbed the steps to the first-floor bar. They stepped inside into an atmosphere redolent with the mingled smells of beer and tobacco and rich spicy food. And the delicious scent of dark coffee beans, roasted and strong.

Juno herself came to greet them. She was a statuesque West Indian woman, easily sixty years old, Rachel estimated, with a long angular body and incongruously dyed purple hair. She was wearing an ankle-length caftan in a multitude of colours, and a curly-headed little girl was propped on one hip.

'Hey, Brody!' she exclaimed when she saw him, and despite her burden she opened one arm and gave him a bone-crushing hug. The child protested loudly, but when Matt bent to speak to her, her lips twitched into a smile before she pushed one thumb into her mouth.

'Hey, Juno.' Matt returned her greeting. 'And this must be Patrice.'

'I'm Megan,' averred the little girl indignantly, and Juno gave her a reassuring cuddle.

'Of course.' Matt grinned at the child, and Rachel felt her stomach lurch at his blatant charm. 'Megan,' he added. 'You're getting so big I didn't recognise you.'

'Smooth-tongued devil,' said Juno in pretend disgust. 'You beware of men like this, Megan. He's all good-looks and no substance.'

Matt laughed. 'You're only jealous, old lady,' he said lightly. 'And you a woman looking half your age.'

'Oh, listen to the man!' Juno turned to Rachel, shaking her head. 'Don't you just love his prattle? But who are you, girl?' She glanced back at Matt. 'I don't think I've seen her before.'

'You haven't.' Matt lifted his shoulders, and Rachel's eyes were drawn to the strong brown column of his throat. 'This is Rachel.' His eyes met hers. 'She's staying at the hotel.'

'You don't say?' Juno studied Rachel's suddenly flushed face with interest. 'Well, she's certainly younger than the one you brought in last week.'

Rachel's jaw dropped then, and she stared at Matt wide-eyed, but his expression didn't change. If the woman's words had disconcerted him, he certainly didn't show it.

'You could be right,' he said non-committally. 'I can always rely on you to keep me in line.'

'As if I could.' Juno was scornful. Then she turned to Rachel again. 'You on holiday, Rachel? Or did this galoot invite you here?'

'Hey, I'm no galoot. I'm a pussycat,' Matt broke in before Rachel could answer her. 'Don't you be putting me down, woman.'

'Ain't no one could put you down, Brody,' declared Juno flatly. 'And you sure as hell ain't no pussycat, neither. A cougar, yeah? Or a jaguar. Anything else, you be kidding yourself.'

'I do that a lot,' replied Matt without rancour. His eyes flickered over Rachel again, and she was sure he could see the uncertainty in her eyes. But she still had no idea what he was thinking when he said casually, 'Well, you have to admit I have good taste.'

'Can't argue with that.' Juno was studying Rachel again with her dark assessing eyes. 'But you look out for this one. She looks fragile. Don't you go breaking her heart, you hear?'

Matt's lips twisted. 'I don't think I could,' he said drily, but Rachel had the uneasy feeling that he might be wrong. Though perhaps not in the way Juno anticipated. There was more than one way to tear a life apart.

'Anyway, I guess you've come for some of my Blue Mountain brew, yeah?'

'Yeah.' Matt nodded. 'Okay if we sit out on the deck?'

'Looks like you got it to yourselves,' agreed Juno. 'You take your ease. I'll see if Oscar's muffins are out of the oven yet.'

'From your lips to God's ear,' said Matt easily, before ushering Rachel ahead of him into the shadowy bar.

The bar was just a way to reach the deck outside. But even at this hour of the morning there were one or two men draped over the bar stools or leaning over a table, enjoying a game of chess. Rachel wondered how they could sit inside on such a lovely morning, but the effort to distract herself with commonplace musings didn't quite come off.

What had Juno meant? What other woman had come here with Matt? And how could she find out if it had been her mother?

Matt directed her to a table overlooking the street. It enabled them to enjoy the view of the harbour, and the flapping canopy overhead protected them from the worst excesses of the sun.

'Like it?' he asked, and Rachel dragged her mind from thoughts of her mother to give a little nod.

'It's very—very—'

'Quaint?' he suggested, arching dark brows, but Rachel shook her head.

'Atmospheric,' she decided firmly. 'It's the kind of place you can imagine pirates gathering to plan their next voyage.'

'Pirates, hmm?' Matt was sardonic. 'I assume you think I'd fit in very well?'

'If the cap fits,' said Rachel lightly, wondering how she could bring the conversation round to more personal matters. 'Juno seems to think you're a bit of a heartbreaker.' She paused. 'Are you?'

'That's for me to know and you to find out,' he remarked, picking up the salt cellar and weighing it in his strong hands. Long fingers shaped the shoulders of the small container, and Rachel felt that careless caress all the way down to her toes.

Then he looked up and found her watching him, and his eyes darkened to a shade of green only found at the bottom of the sea. 'What?' he asked. 'What are you thinking? I can feel your eyes undressing me. Or am I wrong?'

'You're wrong!'

He was always able to disconcert her, and she wished she dared ask him outright if he'd brought her mother here. That might disconcert him, but she couldn't guarantee it. Besides, she was such a wuss she didn't have the guts to do it.

'Okay.' While she'd been worrying over her options, Matt's eyes had remained on her. And now she could feel the hot colour rising up her cheeks. 'Would you like me to undress you instead? I'd enjoy that enormously. I might find an English rose tattooed on your butt.'

'You might not!'

Rachel stared at him angrily, and Matt gave her another considering look. 'You don't like tattoos?'

'I didn't say that.'

'Okay.' His eyes danced. 'I'll show you mine if you'll show me yours.'

Rachel pressed back against the slats of her chair. 'I've seen yours,' she said tightly, and Matt's lips quivered with amusement.

'So you have,' he agreed, sobering. 'Which doesn't seem fair, does it?'

Rachel couldn't look at him. In her mind's eye she could see the outline of the nighthawk very clearly. Indeed, she thought she'd glimpsed it earlier through the thin fabric of his shirt, its dark plumage unmistakable against his skin.

Once again the conversation had got away from her, and she was almost relieved when Juno returned with the coffee he'd ordered.

'Here we go,' she said, setting down two mugs of steaming black liquid. 'Now, I've brought you cream and sugar, Rachel. But I know Matt, here, likes it just the way it comes.'

'Don't I always?' remarked Matt lazily, and Rachel knew it was another comment that could be taken two ways.

'And Oscar's sent you each a pecan and maple syrup muffin,' Juno added, evidently used to his innuendos. She squeezed Rachel's shoulder. 'You try one of these, girl. It'll put a bit more flesh on those bones.'

'She doesn't need any more flesh on her bones.' Matt's protest was good-humoured. 'I think she's perfect the way she is.'

'Well, you be careful, girl.' Juno touched Rachel's shoulder again, almost in warning. 'When he tells you that you're perfect, he wants something. You can be sure of it.'

Rachel didn't have an answer to that, and she was almost as relieved when Juno went away again as she'd been when she'd arrived.

'Try the muffin,' Matt suggested, lifting his own and burying his strong white teeth in the soft sponge. 'Mmm, it's almost worth getting fat for.'

Rachel broke open the muffin in front of her, glad of something to do with her hands. And the smell almost made her salivate. She could easily forget why she'd invited him here. Crispy nuts, maple syrup, and rich fluffy sponge cake. Wonderful!

She nibbled on a corner, wondering how to begin. Then, after adding a slurp of cream to her coffee, she took a sip. As Matt had promised, it was delicious, the caffeine giving a much-needed boost to her psyche.

'Tell me about yourself.'

For a moment Rachel thought she must have conveyed the words by osmosis. But it wasn't she who'd spoken them. It was Matt.

'Tell me about Rachel Claiborne,' he said, watching the play of emotions crossing her face. 'Do you have a job in England? An occupation?'

'Well, I'm not a lady of leisure,' said Rachel tartly, before realising she was not going to get anywhere if she was off-hand. 'I—well, I work for a newspaper.'

Matt regarded her with interest. 'You're a reporter?' he asked. 'What—are you some hot-shot columnist I should have heard of?'

Rachel had to smile then. Shaking her head, she said, 'Nothing so glamorous. I work for the *Chingford Herald*. It's just a local newspaper that mostly survives because of its advertising pages. I work in the advertising department, sometimes on the computer and sometimes on the phone, soliciting customers.'

'Soliciting, hey?' said Matt lazily, taking a mouthful of his coffee and savouring the taste. He grinned. 'Why am I not surprised?'

Rachel's lips tightened. 'Soliciting advertising,' she corrected him primly, and saw the way his lips twitched at her words. 'I'm actually quite good at it.'

'I believe you.' Matt allowed his eyes to drop to her mouth. 'Honestly, I do.'

He was teasing her, she knew, but Rachel was too tense to take it. 'No, you don't,' she retorted angrily. 'You're too busy trying to think of your next gibe. Let me guess: you think the only reason I got my job was because my boss fancied me.'

'No!' Matt groaned. 'I didn't say that. Boy, do you have some opinion of men! What happened? Did some cheap bastard seduce you and let you down?'

Rachel gasped, but when she would have jack-knifed out of the chair Matt's hand shot across the table to grasp her wrist. His fingers were surprisingly cool, but his grip was powerful. Rachel could feel its strength all the way up her arm.

'Calm down,' he demanded, and she was glad the deck was empty. 'What the hell else was I supposed to think when you react like crazy every time someone mentions your looks?' He shook his head. 'You *are* good to look at, Rachel. There, I've said it. So sue me. But I've known dozens of good-looking women who hold down responsible jobs purely on their own merit.'

Rachel felt foolish. 'I bet you have,' she muttered, in an effort to defend herself. But her awareness of him was now stirring like a fire in her belly. And that was bad.

'You have to have the last word, don't you?' he demanded harshly. 'But it may surprise you to know the world doesn't revolve around what you think.'

It wasn't easy, but somehow Rachel managed to drag her

wrist away. 'I never thought it did,' she denied, rubbing the feeling back into her arm. 'I'm sorry if I've offended you again, Mr Brody.' She thrust back her chair. 'I think it would be best for both of us if I just leave.'

'Rachel!'

She'd barely got to her feet before he moved into her path to stop her. Rachel turned then, desperately seeking for another way to get off the deck, and scurried towards the exit. She heard him coming after her, heard his feet thudding across the boards, so that when his arm snaked about her waist she panicked.

She was beating frantically at his arm when he hauled her back against him. 'Pack it in!' he exclaimed, his patience shredding. 'What do you think I'm going to do to you?'

'I don't know, do I?' she countered ridiculously, wondering what had happened to the cool, controlled individual she'd used to be. But as soon as he laid his hands on her all commonsense deserted her.

'Well, you're quite safe with me,' he told her grimly, the muscles of his chest and stomach hard against her quivering form. 'You're not irresistible, Rachel. Whatever you've been led to believe.'

Rachel let out a cry of protest. 'I don't believe I am irresistible. You—you just make me say things I don't mean.'

'And why is that?' he asked, bending his head close to her ear so she could hear the whispered words. 'Could it be because this is what *you* want? And you don't have the guts to ask for it yourself?'

Rachel's breathing constricted. 'Of course not.'

'Sure about that?' He deliberately pushed himself closer, so she could feel the unmistakable pressure against her bottom. 'Really?'

'I'm sure,' she said, but the words wobbled. She could feel his body stirring against her, and the knowledge was exhilarating and terrifying both at the same time.

She had to get away.

''Course, you know I'm enjoying this,' Matt went on roughly. And she suspected he wasn't quite as cool as he appeared when she heard an edge in his voice.

'I'm—sorry.' The words stuck in her throat. She was having to fight the urge to lean back against him. It was years since she'd allowed any man to touch her, and she had to remember her reasons for being here.

She glanced back over her shoulder, and any moisture there'd been in her mouth dried at the predatory gleam in his eyes. 'I—have to go,' she said, but she wondered if she really meant it. The feel of him, the smell of him, the raw male power of his nearness, was enveloping her in an unfamiliar haze of longing. And when his lips brushed her neck she felt as if her body was burning up.

But when his hands moved to her waist she sensed a certain ambivalence. Was he going to pull her even closer, or was he going to push her away? Her sudden intake of breath caused him to hesitate. And every nerve in her body tingled in anticipation of his kiss.

But he didn't kiss her. Instead, although his breath moistened her bare shoulder, it was his teeth that grazed her skin. He nibbled at her neck, pulled a pearl of soft skin into his mouth and suckled greedily. And wetness exploded between her legs as his tongue caressed her. It was as if he was possessing her, and she didn't want him to stop.

When he lifted his head, she felt almost dizzy with longing. She'd forgotten all about where she was, and that they were visible to anyone passing by on the harbour road.

But she didn't move. She wasn't sure her legs would support her if he released her. She just lay against his shoulder, panting, her breasts, her stomach, her thighs, all aching for him to go on.

It was Matt who spoke. 'You said something about leaving,' he muttered in a harsh voice, and Rachel needed several seconds to bring sanity back into focus again.

'I—I did,' she agreed at last. She forced herself to move away from him, knowing she'd made a terrible mistake. Thankfully, her legs did support her. But her whole body had stiffened with the callousness of his rejection.

'Yeah.'

As she turned, Matt ran an impatient hand down over his abdomen. She guessed he was making sure there was no evidence for her to see. 'Finish your coffee,' he said, striding away towards the bar behind them. 'Juno will be offended if you don't empty your cup.'

CHAPTER SIX

MATT drove back to the plantation house with Caleb clinging anxiously to his seat every time the Range Rover skirted the edge of the cliffs or came close to plunging down a ravine. The old man knew his employer was in a foul mood, and knew better than to complain about his driving.

But the breaths he kept sucking in eventually attracted Matt's attention, and he turned to Caleb with an impatient expression.

'What?' he demanded. 'Don't you trust me to get you back to Jaracoba in safety?'

'I wouldn't dream of saying such a thing, Mr Matthew,' said Caleb with dignity. And then, because he couldn't help himself after all, 'Please, sir. Keep your eyes on the road.'

Matt blew out an irritated breath, but he did as the man suggested and slowed the vehicle. He didn't want Caleb making some comment in his father's hearing when they got back to the house.

Nevertheless, he was cursing himself for the way he'd behaved at Juno's. It wasn't good enough to say Rachel had got under his skin—although she had. The truth was, he'd wanted to go a hell of a lot further than he'd permitted himself. And then only a massive effort of will had held him back.

He wasn't supposed to handle the merchandise, he thought bitterly. She was a guest at the hotel, and he'd had no right to touch her. Particularly knowing who she was. But his desire for her had got the better of him—or almost. He couldn't remember ever feeling such an attraction for a woman before.

Which was crazy, in the circumstances. She'd evidently come out here looking for her mother, and she wouldn't thank him for keeping information from her. But Sara had her own reasons for keeping their relationship a secret, and it wasn't really his place to interfere with her plans.

Nonetheless, it bugged him. It would be so much easier if Rachel knew who he was. But then, unless Sara changed her mind about being honest with her daughter, Rachel herself would want nothing to do with him. She would probably be horrified that he'd touched her at all.

Dammit!

He flung the vehicle through the gates of his family's plantation, barely skimming the stone posts as he accelerated past. An avenue of banana trees and coconut palms swept unnoticed by the open windows of the Range Rover, the fragrant scents of the orchids that grew beside the river as commonplace to him as the beautiful plantation house that stood at the end of the drive.

He brought the car to an abrupt halt beside the row of garages. Once these buildings had housed the carriages his ancestors had owned, and his father still retained a horse-drawn buggy that he occasionally used about the estate.

Caleb climbed out gratefully, and Matt pulled a wry face as he handed over the keys. 'I know, I know,' he said. 'You're glad to be back in one piece.'

Caleb's lined face broke into a grin. 'Fastest trip from town I ever made,' he replied humorously. 'Even your daddy never went faster than fifty miles an hour on those roads.'

Matt shrugged. 'What can I say? I'm a better driver than he is. Only don't tell him I told you.'

Leaving the old man laughing, Matt turned away from the garages to approach the house. Massive oak trees shaded the front of the building and Matt vaulted up the steps to the wraparound porch whose roof was supported by a doz⋯ elegant pillars.

Double doors stood wide to the enormous hallway beyon⋯ its polished boards gleaming from a thousand rubbings. Pa⋯ aqua-coloured walls created an atmosphere of lightness, t⋯ larger windows his father had had installed adding to its ai⋯ grace.

To the right of the hall double pocket doors gave acce⋯ to a spacious morning room. And beyond this another do⋯ led into the library, which these days served as his fathe⋯ study as well. To the left, a grand dining room led into a hig⋯ ceilinged sitting room, with his stepmother's music room ⋯ the back of the house.

Although it was already late afternoon, Matt made h⋯ way to his father's study. Giving a light tap on the door, ⋯ entered the room that Jacob Brody had made essentially ⋯ own. Although the stroke he'd had three months ago had l⋯ him partially paralysed down one side of his body, he w⋯ gradually regaining the use of his limbs.

Jacob was seated on a chaise-longue near the open wind⋯ when Matt came into the room. He'd evidently been workin⋯ because his desk was covered with papers. But exhaustion h⋯ got the better of him, and he was taking a well-earned res⋯

His eyes had been drooping when Matt entered the libra⋯ but they opened wide when they saw his son. 'You're late,' ⋯ said, attempting to sit up straight despite the weakness in ⋯ lower spine. 'Did you see Carlyle?'

'Yeah, I saw him.' Matt dropped into the chair at the oth⋯ side of his father's desk. 'He's going to send the shipment ⋯ when the next supply boat arrives. That way it will go straig⋯ to Kingston and pick up the cargo ship from there.'

'Good, good.' His father nodded. 'What with one thi⋯ and another, I've been neglecting my duties.'

'You mean I have,' said Matt drily. 'And the girl's arriv⋯ is just another complication.'

'But I understand you find her quite fascinating,' remarked Jacob quietly.

'Ah. You've been talking to Amalie.' Not for the first time Matt resented his sister's interference. 'We met Rachel on the pier, after I'd checked out the *Bellefontaine*.'

'Rachel?' His father arched dark eyebrows, a mirror image of his son's.

'All right. Ms Claiborne, then,' said Matt sourly. 'A rose by any other name…'

'You think she's an English rose?'

Matt knew Jacob was only teasing him, but after this morning's encounter he couldn't respond in kind.

'Where is Amalie?' he asked instead, changing the subject. 'She's promised to be in for dinner. She wants to talk to me. About her allowance, I assume.'

'She's about here somewhere,' muttered his father vaguely. He still hadn't attuned himself to leaving the family finances to his son. 'Tell me about this girl. Sara's daughter. Is she as attractive as her mother?'

'She's nothing like Sara,' said Matt, not wanting to talk about the two women in the same breath. He flicked the papers lying on the desk. 'How are you getting on with your book?'

Jacob had been writing a history of the island for as long as Matt could remember. But since his stroke it had proved beneficial as a means to stimulate his attention. With Matt taking control of the running of the plantation, and the charter operation as well, Jacob had had plenty of time to review his notes.

The older man shrugged now. 'I haven't been in the mood for it today.'

Matt picked up a picture of a horse-drawn carriage that was to be included in the illustrations. 'That's a pity,' he said, putting one picture down and picking up another. 'These are really good.'

ANNE MATHER

Jacob said nothing and, realising he couldn't avoid th
subject entirely, Matt relented. 'You're not worrying abo
my relationship with Sara, are you?'

'Is there something I should worry about?' Jacob's eye
were shrewd. 'You care about her, don't you? How could
object to that?'

'I don't know.' Matt spoke broodingly. 'And Diana?' H
stepmother had a right to an opinion. This was her hom
too.

'Diana's far too busy arranging this year's music festiva
said her husband drily. 'In any case, she knows you have yo
own life to lead. We can't control who you choose to invite
Mango Key.'

Mango Key was Matt's own house that was situated o
the other side of the plantation, near the ocean. He'd use
to spend a lot of his time there. But since his father's strok
and the increased responsibilities that had put upon him, l
was spending more and more time at Jaracoba. Not that l
minded. He loved the old house that would one day be his.

He scowled now. He'd been so sure he knew what he w
doing. But since meeting Rachel the situation had change
Why would she come out here, obviously looking for h
mother, unless she had a very good reason? What had Sa
told her family before making this trip to renew her acquai
tance with him?

God knew, it was years since he'd seen her. He'd been a b
of barely nineteen when they'd first met in New York. He
been in his first year at Princeton University, and his initi
reaction to the older woman had been mixed.

Even today he wasn't sure if he really liked her. Love
her? Perhaps. But that was suspect, too. Sara had always be
brittle, and now she was bitter. He had the feeling she thoug
the world owed her a living. That she resented the way h
life had turned out.

Whereas Rachel…

But he didn't want to go there. He had no right thinking about Rachel, and she was certainly not someone he intended to discuss with her mother.

However, he would have to tell Sara that her daughter was on the island. That was the least he could do for either of them. He'd put off mentioning it to Sara for days, hoping—probably stupidly—the situation would resolve itself.

But it wasn't going to, and the sooner Rachel confronted her mother and left the island, hopefully taking Sara with her, the better it would be for all concerned. Whatever Sara said, she couldn't stay here.

His scowl deepened. He wouldn't want her to.

Rachel refused to look at the mark on her neck when she got back to the hotel. In retrospect, the scene had been so embarrassing the last thing she needed was a reminder of it.

But then, next morning, she looked into the bathroom mirror and saw it before she remembered what had happened. A dark stain against the still-pale skin of her throat, it was unmistakable. Anyone seeing it would know exactly what it was.

Which had probably been his intention, she thought, touching the mark with tentative fingers. It was hot and it was tender, and it wasn't going away.

If he'd bitten her anywhere else it wouldn't have been half so noticeable. With the slight tan she was acquiring it might have blended in. Not that he'd considered her feelings when he touched her. And the memory of his teeth, moving against her skin, could still bring a shiver of apprehension skimming down her spine.

Dear God, the man was dangerous. But she'd known that. He'd seduced her mother away from her father and now he was attempting to seduce her. He was a predator, as his tattoo announced, totally without conscience. And with all the savage grace of a tiger.

She blew out a breath and reached determinedly for her toothbrush. There was no use crying over spilt milk, as her grandmother used to say. She had to stop fretting about what had happened and concentrate on her reasons for being here. She still hadn't found her mother. That should be her primary concern.

The trouble was, when she'd had the opportunity to find out more about Matt she'd blown it. Her own lack of confidence in herself had ruined the chance she'd had.

If only she wasn't so aware of him. But she wasn't used to dealing with a man who could so easily use her own hang-ups against her. Let's face it, she thought disconsolately, she wasn't used to dealing with a man, period. Particularly not a man like him, who possessed such a raw sexual appeal.

With the mark on her neck blatantly proclaiming its origins, Rachel decided to leave her hair loose this morning. She could hardly cover up with a high-necked sweater, even if she'd brought one with her.

A cropped pink vest and the short pleated skirt she'd worn on her first morning on the island were hardly confidence building. But then, when she'd left England she hadn't known who—or what—she was going to be dealing with.

Slipping wedge-heeled sandals onto her feet, she opened her door and stepped out onto the landing. It was still quite early, barely eight o'clock, but her body was taking longer to adjust to the five-hour time difference than she'd expected.

There was no one about. Apparently even her neighbours weren't up yet. She started towards the stairs and then halted abruptly. The double doors she'd seen Matt coming out of were just along the gallery. If it was his suite of rooms, might her mother be staying there?

It was worth a try, at least. If the doors were locked, so be it. But if they weren't…

They weren't. But when Rachel gripped the handle and opened one of the doors her disappointment was intense. Far from being the cosy love-nest she'd envisaged, beyond the doors was a large office, with printing machines and fax machines and filing cabinets, and a row of desks complete with computers.

Thankfully no one was about at the moment. It was obviously too early for the staff to be working. But she could imagine how embarrassed she'd have been if she'd had to confront a dozen curious faces.

Closing the door again, she hurried away, reversing her steps and heading back towards the stairs.

The lobby was blessedly familiar territory. 'Good morning, Ms Claiborne,' called the receptionist on duty, and Rachel acknowledged the greeting with an automatic smile. Evidently the staff were encouraged to remember the names of the visitors. Probably to promote an illusion of intimacy between themselves and the hotel guests.

Breakfast, thought Rachel, trying to focus on the morning's routine. Then another trip into town on the unlikely off-chance that she might run into her mother. And if that didn't work she was just going to have to ask Matt himself.

She wasn't looking forward to that event. He might not even come into the hotel today. Of course the taxi driver had said the Brodys owned most of the island, so surely it must be possible to get a phone number, at least?

'What in God's name are you doing here?'

Rachel had been heading towards the terrace restaurant when the irate yet absurdly familiar tones arrested her progress. With a feeling of disbelief, she turned on her heels to face the woman who was hurrying to catch up with her.

Her mother!

Who was barely recognisable, even so. In cream flared pants and a flowing smock, a long scarf in orange chiffon floating carelessly about her shoulders, Sara Claiborne looked much different from the woman who'd raised her. Her dark hair, which had been lightly threaded with grey, was now a startling shade of copper. She'd always been an attractive woman, but now her looks were enhanced with eyeshadow and mascara, her full lips painted a glossy shade of crimson.

She looked younger, too, but harder. Obviously she felt it was what she had to do to keep a man like Matt Brody.

Rachel felt sick. She'd wanted to find her mother, but not like this. And it was obvious that the older woman was decidedly less than pleased to see her.

'Mum…'

Rachel managed to get the word out, but when she went to give her mother a hug Sara Claiborne resisted the attempt.

'Come on,' she said shortly. 'What's going on here, Rachel? Oh, don't bother to answer that. I can see it in your face. Your father sent you. I should have known he wouldn't be able to keep his nose out of it.'

Rachel gasped. 'He was worried about you, Mum,' she whispered in protest, glancing anxiously around the lobby, sure that their conversation was being monitored by a dozen pairs of eyes.

'So he sent you here to spy on me, is that it?' Sara seemed to have no such worries. Her lips twisted. 'Really! That man is beyond belief.'

Rachel stared at her in astonishment. Then, with another glance about her, she said, 'Can we continue this in a less public place?'

'Why?' Sara was aggressive. 'I'm only speaking the truth.'

Rachel shook her head. If she'd ever pictured the scene where she found her mother, it had certainly been much different than this. Sara was in the wrong here; it was she who should be apologising to her husband. Instead of which she was accusing them of spying on her.

'Look, Mum—'

'No, *you* look.' Sara spoke tersely. 'I want you to go back to England, Rachel. I don't want you here. And as for the way you've been hanging about the Brodys…' She spoke contemptuously. 'I don't know what your game is, but you're not going to succeed.'

Rachel's jaw dropped. 'I haven't been "hanging about the Brodys" as you put it,' she protested. 'I've just been trying to find you, that's all.'

Her mother used her scarf to fan her flushed face, and then fixed her daughter with a piercing look. 'That's not what I hear from Matt.'

From Matt!

Rachel swallowed back the bile that rose into her throat at this accusation. She couldn't believe it. Matt had been reporting on her to her mother. Had Sara known she was here all this time without even bothering to pick up the phone?

'Well, you're wrong. *He's* wrong,' Rachel declared now, her cheeks burning at the insult. She was surprisingly near to tears, and that infuriated her. 'As for Daddy sending me here—what did you expect, Mum? You run off to the Caribbean to meet a man we don't know, without even telling us when you're coming back.'

'I may not come back.'

The words were spoken quietly enough, but their impact was terrifying. Sara's eyes left Rachel's face and drifted thoughtfully round the lobby. It was as if she was looking for someone, and for the first time Rachel wondered how she'd got to the hotel. Had Matt brought her? Her skin crawled at the prospect. She wanted desperately to escape to her room. She wanted to stay there until her mother had gone.

Which was ridiculous, in the circumstances. Dear God, she'd been trying to find her mother. And now she wished she hadn't. This woman was nothing like Sara Claiborne. She seemed totally self-absorbed, totally self-possessed. She was indifferent to her daughter's—and her husband's—feelings. It was as if the real Sara Claiborne had vanished and left this total stranger in her place.

Rachel caught her arm, unable to prevent herself from re-acting to such a bald statement. Besides, she wanted to be sure she had her mother's attention before she spoke.

'What do you mean?' she exclaimed. 'You might not come back? You have to. Surely you don't honestly believe you can stay here?'

'Why not?' Sara's eyes were distant now. 'I love this island.' She hesitated a moment, and then said slowly, 'I think the only times I've been really happy in my life is when I'm here.'

Rachel took an involuntary step backwards. 'You don't mean that.'

'Oh, I do.'

'But what about Daddy?' She bit back the words, *And me*, but they were tacitly implied just the same.

Her mother clicked her tongue. 'Oh, Ralph,' she said dis-missively. 'You must know that your father and I have been having problems for some time.'

'No!'

'We have.' Sara's voice was flat. 'Ever since your father decided not to retire last year. I only agreed to sell the house and move into that poky apartment because he'd convinced me that it would give us more time and money to spend on holidays and travel. Instead of which he still goes off to work every morning, doing what he wants to do, and I don't even have a garden to distract me.'

Rachel blew out a breath. 'And have you told Daddy this?'

'Only a hundred times.' Sara's lips twisted. 'But he won't listen to me, so why should I listen to him?'

Rachel tried to think. Something else her mother had said suddenly came back to her. 'Have you been to St Antoine before?'

'When I was younger.' Sara was evasive. 'As I say, I love it here. I feel younger here.' Her eyes turned back to Rachel's. 'Is that such a bad thing?'

Rachel didn't know how to answer her. The trouble with being in the middle of something was that you could see both sides. But, whatever her mother said, she couldn't see any future for her with Matt Brody. Her hand strayed guiltily to the bite on her neck. Not when he didn't consider anyone but himself.

'Anyway...' Rachel had been quiet too long, and her mother was getting impatient. 'I don't really care what you think. I suggest you get on the phone and book yourself a flight back to England. If your ticket isn't viable I'll sub you, if you like. Just leave me alone to deal with things my way.'

'But, Mum—'

'And you can stop calling me *Mum* all the time. While I'm here, I'm Sara. That's what Matt calls me and I like it.'

Rachel didn't have an answer. And with a casual wave her mother swung on her heel and started towards the door.

'Don't blame me for wanting a life, Rachel,' she called back over her shoulder.

But Rachel had already turned away.

CHAPTER SEVEN

RACHEL spent the rest of the day in a state of raw confusion.
There was no more need for her to go looking for her mother,
but that was hardly a relief. And she still didn't know where
Sara Claiborne was staying.

After drinking several cups of coffee in lieu of breakfast,
she went up to her room and changed into a swimsuit and
shorts. She couldn't go home, whatever her mother had said.
Not yet. Not until she knew whether Sara was serious about
staying here.

Going downstairs again, she bought a magazine at the hotel
kiosk and settled herself in a lounge chair by the pool. She
knew she ought to have rung her father, but she hadn't the first
idea what she was going to say to him. It was really up to her
mother to sort out her own problems, although the woman
she'd met earlier didn't appear to have any that Rachel could
see.

The whole situation was a nightmare. Watching holiday-
makers splashing about in the pool, Rachel envied them their
freedom. Her situation was so uncertain. And it was all Matt
Brody's fault.

Despite her worries, the day passed remarkably quickly.
She didn't eat any lunch. But she did buy two mugs of the
delicious island coffee from the poolside bar.

She used the sunscreen she'd bought liberally, but her skin

still prickled. She knew she was overdoing it, but somehow sunburn seemed preferable to the torment of her thoughts.

She hadn't had a dip in the pool yet, so in the late afternoon she slipped off her shorts. Then, refusing to feel self-conscious, she crossed the tiled apron surrounding the pool and gazed down into the water.

The smell of the swimsuit reminded her irresistibly of Matt, and she wished she'd brought more than one suit with her. Despite rinsing it thoroughly when she'd got back from the beach, it still retained the tang of the sea.

The pool itself was almost empty. Most of the guests had gone up to their rooms to prepare for the evening ahead. Only two younger children were playing at the shallow end. Rachel had the deeper end to herself.

It looked very inviting and, taking a deep breath, she stretched out her arms and dived into the water. It wasn't exactly cold, but it wasn't warm either. The sun had only heated the surface. Deep down, she felt the chill sting her burning arms.

She came up gasping and swam swiftly from one side of the pool to the other. That felt better. The physical exertion warmed her limbs, and she swam back and forth a couple of times before returning to cling onto the rim.

She was breathless now. The unusual activity had robbed her of any strength. In addition to which she felt slightly dizzy. Probably because she'd had nothing to eat that day.

'Are you trying to kill yourself?'

The harsh masculine voice shouldn't have been familiar, but it was. Lifting her eyes, Rachel let her gaze travel up over formal suit trousers, that still couldn't quite disguise the impressive bulge between his legs, and an equally formal shirt and jacket, black on black. His tie was pearl-grey, the only splash of colour in his outfit. And, despite telling herself that she hated him, Rachel couldn't deny how completely stunning he looked.

'Well?'

He was waiting for her answer, and, dragging her eyes away from such perfection, she dug her nails into the tiles to ground her racing pulse.

'I don't see what business it is of yours, Mr Brody,' she said tightly, knowing the formality of her response would annoy him. 'I was having a swim, as it happens. As I'm sure you've seen for yourself.'

He didn't say anything for a moment, but she could feel his frustration coming off him in waves. And, in spite of her determination not to let him intimidate her, she had to look up at him. If only to assure herself that her words had found their mark.

'How long have you been out here?' he demanded. 'I assume you know your shoulders and arms are sunburned? It's probably just as well you can't see your face.'

'Why?'

'Guess.' He spoke impatiently. 'For God's sake, Rachel, I thought you had more sense.'

'Like my mother, you mean?'

Rachel couldn't resist the accusation, but if she'd expected any defence from him, she was disappointed.

'Let me help you out,' he said instead, bending and offering her his hand.

'I don't want to come out.' It was childish, she knew. Her limbs were already trembling with fatigue and she was beginning to shake.

'D'you want me to come in and get you?'

Rachel caught her breath. 'As if that's likely in that outfit,' she said scornfully. 'Go away, Matt. I don't need your help to get out of the pool.'

'Now.'

'Soon,' she compromised, even if the idea of letting go of the rim again filled her with apprehension.

'Now,' he insisted, and to her horror he took off his jacket.

He dropped it onto the lounge chair she'd been occupying and then returned to the pool-edge to pull off his shoes.

At once, Rachel realised he'd meant what he said when he'd threatened to come in and get her. 'Don't,' she cried, before he could remove the expensive loafers. 'All right. I'll get out. You don't have to continue the charade.'

'It's no charade,' retorted Matt bleakly, making no attempt to move away. 'Give me your hand.'

Rachel felt ridiculously mutinous. 'I don't need your assistance,' she insisted. But when she tried to press down on her hands to swing herself out of the pool there was no strength left in her arms.

Her fingers slipped off the ledge, and her arms flailed helplessly before she found herself sinking beneath the surface. And, because she wasn't prepared for the sudden submersion, her nose and mouth both filled with water.

Oh, God, she was drowning, she thought, momentarily panicking as the water closed over her head. Why couldn't she have acted sensibly and accepted Matt's help when he offered it? Could she do nothing right where he was concerned?

Her feet touched the bottom of the pool at that moment, and somehow she summoned all her strength and pushed upward again. And when she did Matt's hand grabbed one of her arms, bringing her to the surface.

He was kneeling on the side of the pool, and as she choked and gasped and tried to get her breath, he leaned into the water and caught her other arm. Then, getting to his feet, he hauled her unceremoniously out onto the side.

She heard him mutter something under his breath as she lay there panting. She could feel the weight of the water that was inside her, but she didn't have the energy to bring it up. Then, as if aware of her plight, Matt pressed a firm hand down on her stomach, rolling her onto her side as soon as she started regurgitating all the liquid she'd swallowed.

She coughed and coughed, fluid spilling out of her mouth

in such profusion she was sure she must have brought up every drop of liquid she'd swallowed that day. She felt hot, and shivery, and totally humiliated. Dear Lord, could this day get any worse?

Apparently it could.

Just as she was hoping he'd go away and let her die, he reached for his jacket and put it on. Then, to her horror, he bent and lifted her up into his arms.

'Your—your suit,' she croaked in protest, aware that she was soaking wet and probably smelling of vomit. But he didn't seem concerned.

'The suit will clean,' he said indifferently, and she had to admit she was grateful not to have to walk through the lobby. 'You need to get into the shower. You're burning up and shivering all at the same time.'

Rachel knew she ought to protest when he headed for the stairs. She cringed at the curious eyes that followed their progress, though she noticed no one attempted to say a word. It was Matt who said briefly, 'Bring a key, Toby,' to the porter, and she remembered she'd left her bag containing her key card and sunscreen beside the pool.

'Oughtn't I to—?'

'Later,' said Matt tersely, and she guessed he'd known exactly what she was going to say.

Toby overtook them on the landing, hurrying to open her door so that by the time Matt got there he could just carry her into her room. He nodded his thanks to the young porter and Toby said, 'No problem, Mr Brody,' before letting himself out again and closing the door.

Matt set her on her feet and nodded towards the bathroom. 'Do you think you can manage?' he asked, and Rachel wondered what he'd do if she said no.

'I think so,' she said instead. 'Um—thank you. And I'm sorry if I've ruined your suit. Let me at least pay for it to be dry-cleaned.'

'Get your shower,' said Matt, taking off his jacket again and looping it over one shoulder. She guessed he'd done it because the jacket was wet, and probably slimy, too. 'I'll arrange for you to have a meal sent up from Room Service.' And when she would have protested, he added, 'You need to eat. Something sweet, preferably. You've had a shock.'

She didn't argue. She didn't have the energy. And, as Matt seemed prepared to stay until she entered the bathroom, she decided to do as he said. She gave him a tentative smile before closing the door and locking it. He probably thought she was locking it against him, but he couldn't have been more wrong.

She ran the shower warm at first, and then slowly increased the pressure. He was right. The cascade of water did make her feel better, although she thought it might be some time before she entered a pool again. How could she have been so foolish? To risk the chance of sunstroke, and then wear herself out so completely she couldn't get out of the water.

She didn't let herself think what might have happened if Matt hadn't been around to save her. If he hadn't had the strength to haul her out. It was all too awful to imagine. Though she suspected she'd have nightmares for some time to come.

When she eventually emerged from the bathroom, wrapped in one of the white towelling bathrobes that was hung behind the bathroom door, she was feeling much better. Still shaken, but at least the shivery feeling had left her.

The mirror in the bathroom had told a different story, however. Her face, and what part of her arms and legs that had been exposed, were still red and angry-looking. Thank goodness her back hadn't been exposed. She might be able to sleep without too much discomfort.

Her eyes widened when she saw someone had entered the bedroom in her absence. The bag she'd left beside the pool was now lying on the bed. In addition, a serving cart had been left near the windows, its folding leaf extended and laid for one.

Her lips parting in surprise and anticipation, Rachel approached the cart. Silver domes hid a variety of dishes, including grilled fish and poached chicken, boiled green bananas and rice, baked crab and mixed salad. There were sweet things, too: sugary dumplings, a roasted pear torte, and ice cream flavoured with either mango or coconut.

A bottle of wine resided in a cooler, but Rachel doubted she'd drink any of that. The bottled water she found in a chilled compartment was much more appealing, and she drank almost a whole bottle before touching the food.

She tasted the fish and found it a little salty, but the poached chicken went smoothly down her throat. It was absolutely delicious. As, too, were the little dumplings. She tried one with a helping of mango ice cream, and was considering having another when someone knocked at her door.

She was reluctant to answer the door, looking as she did. What if it was her mother? What if Matt had informed Sara of her daughter's near drowning? What if the reason Matt had been so formally dressed was because he was taking her mother out to dinner?

She sighed. It could, of course, be the maid, come to collect the cart. And if she didn't answer would the girl let herself in, thus defeating any decision to ignore the knock?

Pushing back her chair, she padded across to the door and peered through the eyehole. Matt was standing outside, and her heart beat a rapid tattoo in her chest. Obviously she had him to thank for the meal she'd just enjoyed. But she doubted he'd arrived to collect the cart.

Although she was sure he couldn't see her, she stepped back automatically. 'Wh-who is it?' she called, and heard the impatient oath he uttered even through the door.

'You know who it is,' he told her shortly. 'You've been

eyeing me up for the last two minutes. Open the door, Rachel. I've brought some cream to treat your sunburn.'

'Oh!'

Rachel didn't hesitate any longer. Flicking the latch, she opened the door a few inches, keeping mostly out of sight. Matt had changed his clothes, she saw. He was now wearing casual drawstring sweats and a white tee shirt. And, judging by the drops of water sparkling on his hair, he'd had a shower, too.

'Thanks for dinner,' she said, attempting to keep her eyes on the jar of cream in his hand and not on the wedge of brown skin exposed by the low-slung pants. 'I—is that the cream?'

Matt glanced down at the jar. Then up again to meet her nervous eyes. 'Yeah,' he said without expression. 'May I come in?'

Rachel expelled an uneven breath. 'You—er—you were going out for dinner, weren't you?' she ventured, which was hardly an answer. 'I suppose I spoiled your plans.'

'You could say that,' agreed Matt, his eyes moving beyond her. 'Are you going to invite me in, or have you already got company?'

Rachel gasped. 'As if!'

'So?'

'I'm not dressed.'

'I can see that.'

'Oh, well—' Deciding she was as adequately clothed as she'd been that afternoon, Rachel stepped away from the door. 'I suppose you can come in.' How could she refuse when he'd practically saved her life?

He came into the room, immediately making it seem smaller. She hadn't noticed that phenomenon earlier, but then she'd been too shocked to notice much beyond the relief of knowing she was safe.

He glanced about him, his eyes taking in the remains of

the meal she'd consumed, his brows arching at the unopen
bottle of Chablis. Then he closed the door behind him, leani
back against it as his eyes turned back to hers.

'I—er—I liked the chicken,' she said hurriedly, despera
for something to say to normalise the situation. 'And—a
the ice cream. It was scrummy.'

'Scrummy?' His lips twitched. 'I don't think I've hea
that word before. I assume it means you enjoyed it, too?'

'Mmm.' Rachel found herself wrapping the folds of th
bathrobe closer about her. 'I know I thanked you before for
you know—saving my life and all, but I want you to know
do appreciate what you did.'

'Particularly as you were such a prickly little cat?' su
gested Matt drily, straightening away from the door. 'Bu
can't take credit for saving your life. You'd have got out
there somehow. The human need for survival's a powerf
thing.'

'All the same...'

'All the same, you're grateful I was there.' Matt pulled
wry face. 'But not soon enough to save you from burning th
delicate skin.'

Did he really think she had delicate skin?

Rachel found the prospect totally intriguing, before con
monsense surfaced again. But she couldn't help being irresis
ibly aware of the intimacy of him being here, in her room. H
was far too attractive. Far too close.

In an effort to distract herself, she pointed to the jar he w
holding. 'And that's the cream?'

'You asked me that before,' Matt reminded her mildl
'And, yes, once again, this is the cream. It's a special reci
that my grandmother used when she first came to the islan
She was pale-skinned, too, and in those days there were
handy pharmacies with a dozen prescription remedies
hand.'

Rachel put out her and. 'What is it?'

'That would be telling.' Matt looked at the jar, but he didn't give it to her. 'It contains lanolin and witch hazel, and cocoa butter, and a few other ingredients. The housekeeper makes it up whenever it's needed.'

'Well—thank you.' Rachel wished he would just give her the cream and leave. 'I'll be glad to use it.'

'And how to you propose to put it on your shoulders?' Matt demanded tersely. 'Loosen your robe. I'll do it for you.'

'No, I—'

'For God's sake, stop behaving as if a man has never seen you naked before,' he grated. 'I'm only offering to treat your shoulders. You can do the rest yourself.'

Rachel swallowed. She wondered what he would say if she told him that no man had ever seen her naked. Well, not since she was a baby, of course. But pride won out over honesty. She'd embarrassed herself enough as it was.

'Well—all right,' she murmured at last. 'Where do you want me to sit?'

CHAPTER EIGHT

MATT wondered what she'd say if he told her. But he reminded himself that he was here for one purpose and one purpose only: to try and ease her sunburn.

The fact that it was burning him up, too, was not her problem.

'Sit on the side of the bed,' he said a little shortly, watching as she carefully eased the collar of the robe down around her upper arms. He knew she was no more exposed than she would have been in an off-the-shoulder evening gown, but the sight of her red skin caused a tightening in his gut.

She looked so fragile, so vulnerable. He wished he could take the pain from her. But his own skin would never burn like this.

Unscrewing the jar, he hesitated a moment and then sat down behind her. Now the heat of her skin rose irresistibly to his nose. A feminine scent mingled a flowery fragrance with warm perspiration, an essence that he found utterly desirable.

Impatient with his reactions, Matt scooped a smear of the ointment onto his fingers. Then, trying to be gentle, he applied it liberally over her reddened skin. She flinched, as he'd expected, but she seemed to steel herself to suffer his attention. Matt couldn't be sure if it was the sunburn cream she was steeling herself against or him.

He could smell the cream now. The delicious aroma of

cocoa butter heightened his awareness of her tender flesh. His gentle massage became a caress, took pleasure in exploring the bones and angles of her shoulders. But his fingers were now pressing far too firmly into her sensitive skin.

He heard her catch her breath, realised instantly what he was doing. And was disgusted with himself for the way he'd behaved. But, dammit, touching her like this was the purest kind of torment he could imagine. She was so soft, so delicate. He couldn't help himself; he wanted more.

His whole body was suddenly charged with tension. As she allowed the folds of the bathrobe to slip lower, he was gifted with a glimpse of the creamy slopes of her breasts. And his eyes were caught by the mark he'd put upon her that day at Juno's. His body stiffened, tightened, grew hard without any volition on his part.

Seeing the bite, he realised what a mistake he'd made in coming here, in thinking he could ignore the connection between them. Rachel was aware of it. That was why she'd been so reluctant to let him into her room. And now here he was, having the kind of thoughts that should have been left outside the door.

With a grim determination he finished his task and screwed the cap back onto the jar. Then, rubbing his hands together, he removed the last vestiges of the cream. She could manage the rest herself, he thought. He certainly couldn't trust himself to touch her again.

Yet he didn't move. For a few seconds he just sat there, putting off the moment when he would have to leave. Then, unable to prevent himself, he leant towards her and blew gently into her ear.

Her head positively spun round, her eyes registering her shock at the unexpected coolness of his breath. 'Did you—?' She broke off abruptly, obviously seeing her answer in his expression. 'Please—don't,' she whispered huskily, but Matt's eyes were on her mouth.

She had such a sensual mouth, he thought, wide and soft and vulnerable. Doubly so as she struggled to maintain some kind of control over the situation.

'Don't what?' he asked unforgivably. As if he didn't know exactly what she meant. He lifted his hand and allowed one finger to stroke down the side of her neck and across her shoulder. 'Doesn't this feel better? Now that the cream has had a chance to do its work?'

'Matt, please…'

'Let me move your hair out of the way,' he said, taking no notice of her protest. 'We don't want to get it greasy, do we?'

Her hair was still damp from her shower, and it clung silkily to his fingers as he lifted a handful to his face. He opened his mouth and allowed the damp strands to invade his lips, glorying in its softness. And, although he was sure she was desperate to move, his sensuous action forced her to stay where she was.

'Matt…'

'Mmm?'

But Matt wasn't really listening to her. Using his free hand, he tugged the bathrobe lower. And as he did so one hard rosy peak emerged proudly from the cloth. Rachel gasped, and would have quickly covered herself again, but Matt wouldn't let her. Instincts as old as time had him firmly in their grip.

When he released her hair, it tumbled unheeded about her shoulders, and Matt allowed his hands to slide smoothly down her neck. His thumbs brushed her ears, felt the pulse beating rapidly in its hollow, and gave in to the urge to follow a path that led unerringly to her breasts.

Common sense and decency seemed to have deserted him. He hadn't intended to touch her, he told himself, but he couldn't let her go. Not yet. Not while her nipples swelled against his palms and he could hear the uneven tenor of her breathing. And she didn't try to stop him except to say in a shaken voice, 'We shouldn't.'

And, God, Matt knew that. Knew he was probably damning his soul for all eternity by taking advantage of her susceptibility. She was fragile at present, weak and breakable. And this was definitely not a great idea.

But it was useless telling himself this when she was so desirable. He already knew how good she tasted, and he badly wanted to taste her again. But not just her soft skin, all of her. Her palms, the backs of her knees, and most particularly that sensitive place between her legs.

Feeling his own body trembling, he half turned her to face him, only to find her eyes were closed. But she didn't resist when his thumb tugged her lips apart and invaded her sweetness. Or when he bent his head and covered her mouth with his own.

He pushed his hands into her hair, angling her face so he could deepen the kiss, allowing his tongue to push into her mouth. Her eyes opened then, but they were soft and languorous. His tongue sank deeper and her breasts were crushed sweetly against his chest.

Her hand rose to clutch the neck of his tee shirt. Soft fingers invaded his collar, curled with unexpected eagerness into his hair.

'You want this?' he breathed against her neck, his own breathing harsh and staccato.

'I want you,' she admitted huskily, her tongue a sexual invitation, and Matt felt any lingering doubts spinning away.

It was easy enough to propel her back on the bed, to loosen her robe and tug the sides apart. There was a moment when he thought she might stop him. Her back arched upward off the quilt, but then subsided again.

Matt eased himself beside her, bending to flick one of those delicious nipples with his tongue. She sucked in a breath and he was struck by how sensitive she was. She was so responsive. He'd never met a woman like her before.

He couldn't help himself. His eyes drifted down over her body. She lay there, legs pressed tightly together, gazing up at him with wide trusting eyes. She was definitely a blonde, he noticed, and then put such thoughts aside. His interest went far beyond the colour of her hair.

She was amazing, he thought. Full breasts, slim and yet rounded hips, long shapely legs. Legs he could already imagine wound around him. And a waist he could span with his two hands.

'You're beautiful,' he said a little thickly, trailing wet kisses across the slight mound of her stomach. He felt her flinch again when he explored her navel with his tongue, and was briefly diverted. She was either very tense or very nervous. He knew she'd had a tough day, but he wanted her to relax.

Then she said, 'Oh, please...' and Matt gave a soft laugh as he looked down at her.

'I intend to,' he assured her huskily. 'Do you mean you or me?'

Rachel shook her head and he returned his attention to her breasts, lifting them into his hands with an unexpected sense of possession. Then he bent to curl his tongue about their swollen peaks.

When he pulled one into his mouth and sucked strongly, he heard her give a soft whimper. But it wasn't a whimper of pain, it was one of pleasure.

'You like that?' he asked, lifting his head and looking at her through his lashes.

'I—like,' she got out unsteadily, her hands reaching for his shoulders, her nails digging almost painfully into his flesh.

Matt expelled a hoarse breath. God, he wondered incredulously, was this woman for real or what? He couldn't ever remember wanting a woman so badly. His erection was almost painful, and he was so glad he'd changed into the loose-fitting sweats.

His hands left her breasts to curve possessively over her hips. He raised one of her legs to bestow a lingering kiss behind her knee and the unmistakable scent of her arousal rose hotly to his nostrils. His hand slid along her thigh, cupped the provocative curve of her bottom, found her damp cleft and allowed his fingers to probe the honeyed curls of her mound...

And then someone knocked at the door.

'Dammit!'

Matt swore more forcefully under his breath, but there was no way he could ignore the summons. The door was closed, but it wasn't locked. And besides, all the housekeeping staff had keys.

His dark eyes met Rachel's startled ones, but she was already wrapping her robe about her, drawing up her legs and huddling back against the headboard behind her. It was obvious what she was thinking; she was probably grateful for the interruption. But Matt had to stifle his frustration as he pushed himself abruptly to his feet.

Crossing to the door, he swung it open with scarcely concealed impatience. It was one of the maids, as he'd suspected, but her eyes widened anxiously when she saw her employer.

'I—er—I've come to turn down the bed,' she said, and Matt was glad his bulk blocked her curious view.

'Thank you, but Ms Claiborne doesn't require your services this evening,' he said.

'Perhaps some towels?' the girl suggested, and Matt wondered if she knew how dangerously she was pushing her luck.

'Nothing,' he said shortly, his eyes brooking no argument, and with another futile attempt to see beyond him the maid turned regretfully away.

Matt closed the door, but for a moment he didn't turn

to look at Rachel. Bracing his hands against the panels, he knew without asking that the maid's intrusion had destroyed any intimacy between them. They were back to square one, and perhaps it was just as well, he thought broodingly. This could have been a mistake. And one he might not be able to dismiss.

Steeling his features, he turned, and found she had left the bed to stand beside the windows. The bathrobe was now securely in place again, her hair twisted into a single coil at her nape.

'You heard that?' he said, and she gave him a brittle little nod over her shoulder.

'Perfect timing,' she said tightly. 'Are you leaving now?'

Matt's smile was bitter. 'Is there any point in my staying?'

Rachel shook her head. 'Probably not.'

'That's what I thought.' Matt picked up the jar of cream from the bed and dropped it onto her night table. 'Don't forget to put some of this on your arms and legs. However they feel now, they will feel worse in the morning.'

'Thank you.'

'My pleasure.' Matt's lips twisted and he turned towards the door. 'And it has been,' he added, disregarding the ache of thwarted arousal. 'Get a good night's rest. It's been a long day.'

Rachel did not sleep well.

As soon as Matt had gone, she'd hurried across the room and locked the door. Not that she expected to be disturbed again. But the action offered a sense of security she'd totally lost.

And, despite being exhausted after all the physical and emotional stimulus of the day, she couldn't rest. She tossed and turned for hours, wondering what she'd have done if the maid hadn't interrupted them. What had she been thinking?

Had she even been thinking? Or had Matt's demands on her senses reduced her brain to a quivering lump of mush?

Perhaps.

She knew she'd totally forgotten her reasons for making this journey. She hadn't thought about her mother, or her father, or what any relationship she might have with Matt would do to them.

Particularly her mother, she conceded, half guiltily, aware that, however reprehensible her mother's behaviour might have been, she evidently cared about Matt. As evidence: the fact that she'd virtually ordered Rachel to leave the island. It wasn't her fault that her daughter was as susceptible to the man as she had been herself.

Rachel's only excuse was that the events of the day had left her reeling. And the gratitude she'd felt towards Matt had made her vulnerable in a way she'd never been before. How was she expected to understand feelings that went beyond anything she'd ever experienced? How could she cope with a man who was as unpredictable as he was beautiful?

But that was too simple an explanation for what had occurred. She'd always been able to control her emotions in the past, so why couldn't she control them now? Something had changed. Something she dared not examine. Since meeting Matt, common sense seemed to have deserted her.

She'd wanted him. There was no doubt about that. For the first time in her life she'd understood the emotional needs that had so far been denied to her. She'd wanted to give herself to him. She hadn't cared about losing control, or losing her virginity. Those things had meant nothing at that moment. She'd wanted to take what he was offering and run with it, to find out at last what she'd been missing all these years.

Or not.

She was fully aware that the experience might not live up to her expectations. When she was at school, she'd decided she wasn't a sexual person at all. Despite her appearance—and the fact that boys thought she must be gagging for it—Rachel had had no difficulty in keeping amorous youths at bay.

Unfortunately, as she'd grown older she'd realised that those early experiences had helped to establish the pattern of her life. She'd had male friends, but she'd never allowed any of them to get close to her. She'd enjoyed their company, their conversation, but as soon as some commitment was needed Rachel had quickly moved on.

And as for love...

How arrogant she'd been, she thought as she lay sleepless, pummelling her pillow continuously, trying to find a comfortable place to lay her head. She'd been foolish to make such a sweeping assumption about her future. Just because she'd never met a man she wanted to go to bed with, it didn't mean he wasn't out there somewhere.

Someone like Matt...

She was up and dressed early the next morning. Her hair, untamed after her shower the night before, now curled riotously to her shoulders. There were lines around her eyes, not surprisingly after the restless night she'd spent, and her lips looked faintly bruised from Matt's sensual mouth.

She touched her lips with fingers that trembled slightly. But then, seeing the weakness, she dragged her hand away. Okay, she was a virgin, but thankfully Matt didn't know that. And if she did see him today she was going to have to pretend he hadn't just blown her mind.

She didn't think she would see him, though. He had no doubt had second thoughts about what had so nearly happened last night, just as she had. She recalled how he'd stood and stared at the door after the maid had departed. It was as if he'd been steeling himself to tell her he was leaving, too.

She shouldn't have been surprised. Dear God, his involvement with her had obviously gone far further than he'd intended. It was all right telling herself that she was doing it for her father, but was she? How far was she prepared to go to save her parents' marriage?

After brushing her hair and securing it with a scrunchie, she examined her arms and legs. The skin still looked a bit angry, but the cream Matt had given her had definitely helped. The burning sensation had almost completely gone.

Then she stepped out onto her balcony, trying to regain the optimism she'd felt when she first arrived on the island. The warmth, the atmosphere, the promise of another beautiful day, were appealing. If only she could concentrate on why she was really here.

Below her, the seductive beauty of the pool mocked her reasoning. It held so many connotations, not least the recollection of what had happened the night before in this room. It was impossible to escape those memories. She had the feeling they'd stay with her for the rest of her life.

Her stomach clenched. If she did see Matt again, how was she going to face him? Recalling the way he'd seen her, on the bed behind her, she felt sick. He might have been just as involved as she had, but he hadn't been naked. Somehow that made everything worse from her point of view.

Still, it was just as well he had had his clothes on when the maid had knocked at the door. She had little doubt that their being together, alone, in her room had not gone unremarked by his staff. She could only hope that the fact that Matt had practically followed the woman downstairs would silence the gossips. Was there a chance that her mother might hear about it, too?

Oh, God!

Thinking about her mother aroused other concerns. She was fairly sure Sara Claiborne would contact the hotel this morning, just to make sure that Rachel had checked out. And when she found she hadn't, could Rachel expect another visit? And if she did appear, what was Rachel going to say?

She decided to wear a simple chemise dress in island cotton. It was navy, with purple flowers, and she'd bought it on her first trip into town when she'd realised that her wardrobe was fairly limited. The colours helped to tone down her sunburned arms.

She spent a few minutes tidying her room before going down for breakfast. She had no desire to be the first person in the restaurant, particularly as she had no appetite to speak of. But she needed to think, to marshal her defences, just in case her mother turned up again. And she'd do that so much better, she thought, with a couple of cups of strong black coffee inside her.

Thankfully, there were several other guests already occupying the tables on the patio. One or two of them acknowledged Rachel, and she managed a friendly wave of recognition. Although it was only a little after eight, people did seem to get up earlier here. Probably to get out and about before the heat of the day sucked all their energy.

She'd drunk three cups of coffee and managed to swallow half an English muffin when someone spoke to her.

It was a male voice, and she instantly thought of Matt. But the young man standing beside her table was a stranger. Well, not a complete stranger, she admitted honestly. He and his partner were two of the people who'd waved to her when she'd first come down.

'Hi,' he said, putting a hand on the back of the chair opposite, evidently waiting for an invitation to sit down.

But Rachel didn't respond to his silent question. She merely raised her face to his and forced a small smile. 'Hi,' she returned, and then dropped her eyes to her plate again, in the hope that he'd get the message. He was already one of a couple. So what was he doing talking to her?

He didn't move away. Instead, he said, 'Are you enjoying your holiday?'

Rachel was tempted to tell him she wasn't on holiday,

exactly, but that would require too much explanation. 'Very much,' she replied, in what she hoped was a quelling tone. Then, pushing back her chair she got purposefully to her feet.

She was preparing to give him another smile and move away, but he blocked her exit.

'You're on your own, aren't you?' he persisted. 'Luce and I saw you sitting by the pool yesterday. We wondered if you'd like to join us for the morning. We've booked one of those boat trips that take you to a secluded cove where you can swim and snorkel. They offer you a picnic on the beach, as well.'

Rachel immediately felt guilty. Was she so conceited that she'd mistaken a friendly gesture for a pass?

'I—well, that's very kind of you—'

'If you've got something else planned, then that's okay.' Had she?

The answer was a definite no. Short of making another trip into town to try and find out where her mother was staying, she had no plans. There was nothing to stop her from joining them, and it might be fun.

'I don't have anything else planned,' she admitted, glancing across the patio to where his partner was waiting. The girl waved, and any lingering doubts Rachel might have had faded away. 'Thank you. I'd be happy to join you. What time are you leaving?'

'About nine.' The man grinned. 'My name's Mark Douglas, by the way. And that's my wife, Lucy.'

'Oh—well, I'm Rachel Claiborne.' Rachel gave the girl another awkward wave. 'I'll meet you in the lobby, right? I just need to collect a few things from my room.'

Most particularly sunscreen, she thought. She wasn't at all sure that going out in the sun again was the most sensible thing to do.

But it was only for the morning...

'Great.'

Mark looked pleased, and although Rachel knew she ha
no reason to feel apprehensive she hoped she wasn't makin
a big mistake. And not just about going out in the sun, sh
thought anxiously. But, for heaven's sake, they were going o
a boat with a lot of other people. And his wife didn't look th
type to allow her husband to play around.

CHAPTER NINE

To BEGIN with, Rachel enjoyed the outing.

It was so good to be with people who knew nothing about her. Who accepted her story that she'd planned to come on holiday with a girlfriend, but the friend had been taken ill at the last moment and been unable to come.

And Mark and Lucy were a nice couple. Mark did most of the talking, but Lucy seemed not to mind. A placid girl, with long dark hair and pretty features, she seemed quite content to leave everything to him.

It was only when her husband went to talk to the skipper of the vessel that she confided to Rachel that they were on their honeymoon. She became quite animated when she described the elaborate wedding dress she'd worn.

They anchored off a small cove, and most of the young people on board dived into the water and swam to the beach. The older members of the party were ferried ashore in a dinghy. Then time was allotted for swimming and snorkelling before a picnic lunch was served.

The food wasn't great, but the scenery was spectacular. In any case, Rachel wasn't hungry. Despite her determination to leave her problems behind her, she couldn't help thinking about her father. What was she going to tell him the next time she called?

Chewing on a skewer of jerk chicken and pimento, she wondered what Matt was doing today. Probably making up with her mother, she mused ruefully. She hoped he wouldn't bring Sara to the hotel.

So far, they hadn't actually discussed his association with her mother. She would find it hard—no, make that *impossible*—to bring the subject up. How could she ask him his intentions towards the other woman when she herself was in such an impossible situation?

They sailed back into the harbour soon after three o'clock. It was later than Rachel had expected, and she could feel her skin prickling with the heat. She had taken precautions, covering her arms and legs with sunscreen as soon as she came out of the water, staying under the parasols the ferry company had provided while she ate her lunch. But the sun was relentless.

Still, it had been a nice day. It had kept her away from the hotel for over six hours and that was good.

It was only as they were driving back to the hotel that Rachel was forced to review her opinion of Mark Douglas. He'd hired a buggy for the duration of their stay on the island, and it was this they'd used that morning to get down to the quay.

Rachel had been seated in the back, of course, but on the return journey Lucy had insisted that she should take the front seat beside Mark.

'It's only fair,' she said easily. 'I'm quite happy to sit in the back.'

Rachel would have been quite happy to sit in the back, too. But it would have been churlish to refuse the young woman's offer.

So, despite some misgivings, she climbed into the front of the buggy, aware that the beach wrap she'd had to put on over her wet swimsuit clung to her body like a second skin.

The first half of the journey passed without incident. It wasn't far from the harbour to the hotel. And, although it was hot, the breeze generated by the open-topped vehicle was welcome relief.

Rachel was happily anticipating the shower she intended to take as soon as they got back when Mark's hand suddenly landed on her bare thigh.

She was horrified. What in God's name was he thinking? His new wife was sitting happily behind them, totally unaware of what was going on.

Sucking in a startled breath, she pushed his hand away, her eyes turning angrily in his direction. 'Do you mind?' she mouthed, not wanting to upset Lucy. She was half inclined to ask him to pull over so she could get out.

'Ooh, sorry!'

If Mark thought the leer of apology he cast in her direction was sufficient, he was very much mistaken. Rachel was fuming, wishing desperately that she'd refused his invitation in the first place.

'I'm not used to driving a stick shift,' he continued, gripping the gearstick ostentatiously. As if he expected her to believe he'd made a mistake.

'What's wrong?'

Lucy had evidently picked up the tail-end of this exchange. But Mark wasn't about to let Rachel give her an explanation.

'Oh, it was just me, bumping Rachel's leg with the gearstick,' he said blandly. 'Sorry about that, Rachel. You've got such long legs, I must be feeling confined.'

Rachel's lips tightened. 'No problem,' she said, hoping he didn't think she bought that apology. She couldn't wait to get out of the buggy.

At the hotel, Lucy got out with obvious enthusiasm. 'Oh, I have enjoyed today,' she said happily. 'You'll have to come with us again, Rachel. I know we'd both love to have you.'

Rachel's smile was forced, but she could hardly blame Lucy

for her husband's crassness. 'Thank you for asking me,' she said politely. 'Would you pass me my bag?'

'I'll get it.' Mark jumped out of the buggy at once, folding the seat forward to reach into the back. 'You go ahead, Luce,' he said. 'I'm going to have myself a beer before I get my shower. You can use the bathroom first.'

'Oh, okay.' Lucy was clearly used to this arrangement. 'See you tomorrow, Rachel,' she called, waving her hand as she walked into the hotel.

I don't think so, thought Rachel, turning to take her rucksack from Mark with every intention of following her. But it was a shame that Mark's behaviour had spoilt the day.

However, he kept a firm hold on her bag, even after his wife was out of sight. 'Why don't we both have a drink together?' he suggested silkily. 'I'm sure you must be ready for something stronger than root beer.'

Rachel caught her breath. 'No, thank you.'

'Oh, come on.' Mark narrowed his eyes. 'I know you like me. I've seen you watching me when you thought Luce wasn't looking. I'm sure she bought all that girlish outrage in the buggy, but you don't have to pretend now. She's gone, babe. You can be yourself.'

Rachel could hardly speak. She *was* outraged. How dared he think she would be prepared to go anywhere with him?

'Just give me my bag,' she said, keeping her tone neutral. 'I want to go up to my room.'

'Why don't you show me your room?' he proposed eagerly. 'Don't be coy, babe. We're both adults. You know I can give you a good time.'

Rachel's gaze was unbelieving. 'You've got to be joking,' she exclaimed, her anger showing. 'Please—give me my bag. I don't want to have to report you to the staff.'

'You wouldn't do that.' He was so smug Rachel wanted to slap him. 'Luce likes you. How do you think she'll feel when

I tell her you've been coming on to me? And I warn you, babe, it's not you she'll believe.'

'Don't call me babe!'

It was all Rachel could think to say. This shouldn't be happening, she thought helplessly. She'd done nothing, absolutely nothing, to encourage him to think—

'Is something wrong here?'

The voice was so memorable. It shouldn't have been, but it was. Rachel turned her head and saw Matt Brody approaching them, his expression revealing nothing of his thoughts.

He seemed so painfully familiar. Although she'd only known him for a few days, she already felt as if he'd always been part of her life. In dark linen pants and a black body shirt, he looked both powerful and intimidating. And when he met her eyes there was so much sexual chemistry in his gaze that she felt its kindling deep inside her.

It was Mark who spoke first. 'No, Mr Brody, nothing's wrong.' He handed Rachel her bag. 'Rachel joined Luce and me on one of those picnic cruises around the island, and we were just saying we'll have to do it again.' His eyes turned to Rachel. 'Isn't that right?'

Rachel pressed her lips together for a moment. Then she said tightly, 'That's right.'

'Maybe tomorrow, hmm?' Mark was persistent. 'I'll get Luce to give you a ring in the morning. Or perhaps you'd like to join us for dinner tonight?'

'No, thanks.'

Somehow Rachel got the words out, but inside she badly wanted to scream. Did Matt believe him? Was that speculative look he was wearing a signal that he suspected neither of them was telling the truth?

'Excuse me...'

Rachel couldn't take any more. Uncaring what either of them thought of her, she ducked her head and hurried across the forecourt and into the hotel. Her flip-flops smacked against the tiles, attracting attention she could very well do without. But at last she reached the stairs and climbed quickly up to her room.

Sagging back against the door, she breathed a sigh of relief. Dear God, what an awful end to what had been a fairly pleasant day. And she didn't kid herself that Mark's pursuit of her was over. She'd met men like him before, and she knew it would take more than one refusal to put him down.

The phone rang as she was going into the bathroom. Her father, she thought wearily. He'd probably been trying to reach her all day. If she told him what she'd been doing he'd assume she was wasting her time.

She couldn't ignore it, however, and, picking up the receiver, she said, 'Yes?'

'Rachel?'

It wasn't her father. Her legs gave out on her and she had to sit down on the bed.

'Yes,' she said, unable to think of any reason Matt might be calling her.

'Have you any plans for dinner?'

Plans? Rachel pulled a wry face. How could she have any plans?

And then understanding came to her. This was Matt's way of finding out if she'd really meant what she said when she'd refused Mark's invitation.

Indignation souring her voice, she said tartly, 'No. I have no plans. I intend to order a meal from Room Service. Then I'm going to have an early night.'

'Are you tired?'

Matt sounded sympathetic, but she resented his enquiry even so. 'No, I'm not tired. And nor am I having a secret tryst with Mark Douglas. I assume that's what you're getting at, but the man's a moron. I wish I didn't have to see him again.'

'Yeah.' Matt sounded amused. Did he believe her? 'That was my impression, too. I hope you don't mind, I told him we

were seeing one another. I let him think we'd had a disagree-
ment, and that was why you were on your own.'

Rachel blew out a breath. 'You didn't!'

'I did.' Matt waited a beat. 'Did I do wrong?'

'Heavens, no!' Rachel's relief was heartfelt. 'I didn't know
how I was going to convince him to leave me alone.'

'Yeah, I got the picture.' Matt's acceptance was such a
godsend Rachel wanted to cry. 'So, if you've no plans and
you're not tired, how about having dinner with me?'

Rachel sniffed. 'You don't have to do this, you know. I
mean—I'm sure Mark's a coward. Now that you've sort of—
staked your claim, he probably won't bother me again.'

'I know that.' Matt's tone was easy. 'But I want to. Are you
still set on having an early night?'

Rachel's heart was beating so fast she was sure he must be
able to hear it. Dear Lord, after last night she'd been sure Matt
would never want to see her again. And that was without the
guilt she felt over both her mother and her father. What sense
was there in pursuing this relationship when it could only end
in tears?

'I—what time were you thinking of having dinner?' she
ventured, despising herself for even considering his offer.
Unless she was going to ask him about her mother, she had
no right to see him at all.

And could she do that over dinner?

Why not?

'How about if I picked you up about six-thirty?' he said
casually, evidently expecting her to agree.

'Um—six-thirty.' Rachel licked her lips, mentally assessing her wardrobe. 'Well, all right.' She paused. 'I'll meet you
downstairs.'

Matt gave a soft laugh. 'Don't you trust me to come up?'

Actually, it was herself she didn't trust, but she wasn't going
to tell him that. 'I'll see you later, then,' she said, and, without

giving him another chance to disconcert her, she put down the receiver.

With at least two hours to spare, Rachel took a leisurely shower. She washed her hair, too, and tried to give it some shape with the hand-drier the hotel provided. But without the right tools it wouldn't do what she wanted. So, giving up, she coiled it into a knot on top of her head.

What to wear was easier, because she'd only brought a limited number of garments with her. She hovered over skinny leggings, worn with a silky top, but decided the leggings might irritate her already hot legs.

She finally decided on a simple wrap dress of silk jersey. It was only thigh-length, and inclined to cling, but because it was black it wouldn't draw attention to her sunburn. A broad patent belt cinched her narrow waist, and she slipped matching heels onto her bare feet.

Her only concession to make-up had been the bronze shadow that coated her lids. And a similarly subtle lip gloss to give her mouth some colour. A handful of gold bangles around her wrist, and the amethyst pendant and earrings her parents had given her on her eighteenth birthday, and she was ready.

She looked smart, she thought, but not over-dressed. All the same, she hoped they weren't eating in the restaurant downstairs. She would hate to have another run-in with Mark Douglas.

When she went downstairs at precisely half-past-six Matt was waiting in the lobby. She'd half expected him to be wearing a suit, as he had the evening before, but his pleated khaki pants and cream linen shirt were definitely informal.

He looked every bit as attractive as he'd done earlier, moving with a lithe, cat-like grace to meet her at the foot of the stairs. His shirt was unbuttoned at his throat, and the khakis shaped his narrow hips and the powerful length of his legs.

She'd never known such a disturbing man, or one who wore his sexuality so easily. She was always aware of it, always aware of him. Yet, despite what had happened the night before—or maybe because of it—she was still so unsure of herself with him.

'A punctual woman,' he remarked drily. 'How unusual is that?'

'I'm always punctual,' replied Rachel primly, refusing to admit that she'd been ready and waiting for the past fifteen minutes. 'Are we dining in the hotel?'

'As you did last night, you mean?'

Matt's green eyes mocked her determination not to think of the way he'd seen her the night before. Naked, body splayed, one leg raised so he could bestow a lingering kiss behind her knee.

She felt a quiver of anticipation run over her. Oh, God, he'd been sucking on her nipple, his hand cupping her bottom. There was no way she could put that image out of her mind.

In an effort to distract herself, she said, 'I wanted to thank you again for what you said to Mark Douglas. I was dreading seeing him again.'

'Yeah, I know,' said Matt, reaching for one of her hands and tugging her gently towards the exit. 'If he troubles you again, just let me know.'

As if she could do that!

Rachel shook her head, but she didn't say the obvious. She didn't know where to reach him, except through the hotel. And she could imagine the speculation there would be if she asked one of the receptionists for his address.

And there was still her mother...

Somehow she had to find a way to ask him about his association with Sara Clairborne. Why, if they were only friends, hadn't her mother told her father what she was going to do? And the claim Sara had made about staying on the island. She couldn't have done that without some support from Matt.

Rachel's mind was buzzing, and it was almost a relief when Matt directed her to his Jeep. Obviously, wherever they were dining, it wasn't within walking distance.

It was almost completely dark, and the night was filled with the sound of cicadas. The atmosphere was warm and slightly humid, the air velvet-soft against her heated skin.

Matt helped her into the front of the Jeep and then walked round to get in beside her. His arm brushed hers as he settled in his seat, and her mouth went dry. She couldn't help it. Her eyes were drawn to the taut thigh only inches away across the console, the unmistakable bulge of muscle between his legs.

She so wanted to touch him. Every nerve in her body was on high alert, responding to his sensual appeal. The goosebumps that ran down her arms and legs were a silent acknowledgement of the effect he had upon her. She'd never experienced such an awareness of her own body, this shameless desire to give herself to him.

She sucked in a breath and he glanced curiously towards her. 'Are you all right?' he asked, and she wondered what he'd say if she told him exactly what she was thinking.

But, 'Fine,' she managed, her voice a little higher than it should be. 'Um—' She cleared her throat, trying to get control of her emotions. 'Where are we going? Is it far?'

'Not too far,' said Matt, which was hardly an answer.

She didn't know the island, so she had no idea what 'not too far' might mean. She tried to remember if they'd passed any restaurants that morning when he'd taken her to Mango Cove. But if they had she'd been too absorbed in other things to notice them.

When they left the small town behind, the road ahead of them seemed awfully dark. Rachel was used to driving in England, where even on the darkest roads there were houses or pubs, small villages. All she could see at present were tall hedges, or the startled eyes of the occasional small rodent attracted by the headlights of the Jeep.

As her eyes adjusted to the darkness, however, she glimpsed the ground falling away at the side of the road. And, because she was nervous, she found herself saying, 'Couldn't we have gone to Juno's again? I liked it there.'

'Did you?' Matt didn't sound as if he believed her. 'And, yes, we could have gone to Juno's, but I thought you might like to see Jaracoba.'

'Jaracoba?' Rachel's mind went blank. Was that the name of a place, or what?

'It's my father's house,' said Matt, glancing her way. 'As a matter of fact, he invited you to dinner.'

CHAPTER TEN

'Oн!'

Rachel couldn't hide her disappointment. She'd thought Matt had invited her to have dinner with him, but now it seemed she'd been mistaken.

Yet wasn't this what she wanted? she argued with herself. An opportunity, perhaps, to confront him with her mother's reasons for being here?

'Don't get me wrong,' Matt continued, evidently sensing her ambivalence. 'It was at my instigation. Though I have to say my father wanted to meet you, too.'

'Why?'

The darkness gave Rachel the courage to be forthright. She doubted she'd have been so brave if Matt had been able to see her face.

'What do you want me to say?' Matt shrugged, glancing her way again, and, remembering the terrain, Rachel wished he'd keep his eyes on the road. 'Because you're Sara's daughter, I guess. He's known your mother for a lot of years.'

'He's known my mother…?' Rachel's breathing was suddenly suspended. 'Is—is your father's name Matthew Brody, too?' she asked, hoping against hope that this was the explanation for her mother's flight.

'No. Jacob,' said Matt, instantly killing that suspicion. He turned between tall gateposts. 'Welcome to Jaracoba.

My great-grandfather founded this plantation over a hundred years ago.'

But Rachel was so tense she hardly heard what he was saying. Her mind was focussed on the evening to come, and she dreaded the possibility that her mother might be here. She didn't want to see her with Matt, whatever their relationship. She was going to speak to him, she reminded herself. Just not like this.

The rasping sound of the tree frogs added to the chorus of the insects. There were fireflies buzzing amongst the trees, like tiny winking lights. But even the glorious scent of frangipani and night-blooming jasmine couldn't distract her. Why had Matt brought her here when he must know she wouldn't be welcome?

The house, when they reached it, briefly diverted her. It reminded her of pictures she'd seen of plantation houses in the southern United States. Painted white, with dark brown shutters and a wraparound porch, it was very impressive. Floodlights illuminated the front of the building and drew attention to the vine-draped balcony and the stately grace of its pillared façade.

Rachel lifted her hands and pressed her fingers to her lips as she gazed at the building. She'd guessed Matt's home would be beautiful, but she hadn't expected anything quite so magnificent as this.

'Do you like it?' Matt asked, turning off the Jeep's engine but making no attempt to get out of the vehicle. He ran the backs of his knuckles down her cheek, and she stiffened instinctively. 'Don't be so apprehensive. Pa's not a frightening man.'

Rachel swallowed. 'You should have told me where we were going.'

'Why?' Matt's dark brows arched. 'Would you have refused to come?'

Would she?

Her tongue circled her lips, unknowingly provocative. 'Will—will my mother be here?'

'No.' Matt spoke without hesitation.

Then, lifting his hand again, he probed her lips with his thumb. And Rachel couldn't stop herself. She bit down on the sensitive pad.

'Ow,' he howled, half humorously. Then, his eyes darkening, 'Promise to do that again later, when we're alone.'

'Will we be alone later?' Rachel couldn't prevent the question.

'Depend on it,' said Matt, his voice thickening, and before she could anticipate what he planned to do he'd pressed a hard kiss to her mouth.

'Good evenin'.'

The deep voice made Rachel jump. She'd been staring at Matt, bemused by the raw possession in his mouth, and it was an effort to turn her head and face the elderly West Indian man who was standing beside her door.

'Sorry to disturb you, Mr Matt,' he said, with some irony in his voice. 'But Mr Jacob, he heard you arrive and he's gettin' impatient, yeah?'

'Yeah, yeah.'

It was with an obvious effort that Matt pushed open his door and thrust his long legs out of the Jeep. Meanwhile, the man opened Rachel's door and said, 'Welcome to Jaracoba, Ms Claiborne.'

Rachel managed a smile. 'Thank you.' She allowed the man to assist her to alight. 'I'm—happy to be here.'

'Aren't you, though?' Matt was at her side now, his hand possessing her arm with undisguised ownership. His eyes mimicked her courtesy. 'This is Caleb, by the way. He's been here since my grandfather's time. Isn't that right, Caleb?'

'Surely is,' Caleb responded good-humouredly. 'Your father and Ms Diana are in the sitting room. Maggie'll be serving dinner in about fifteen minutes. That okay?'

'Whatever you say,' said Matt, guiding Rachel towards the flight of steps that led up to the porch. 'I guess we'll have time to get a drink.'

Despite her awareness of the strong fingers wrapped around her arm, Rachel couldn't help admiring the beauty of the old building. There were dark bamboo chairs and benches on the porch, each upholstered in a pretty navy and white striped pattern. There were planters filled with climbing plants and pots spilling fragrant shrubs across the polished boards of the floor.

Rachel guessed it would be an ideal place to sit on a hot day, but before she had a chance to take it all in Matt was leading her through a cool tiled hall and into a formal dining room.

She saw a table that could easily seat a dozen guests, gleaming with silver and crystal. Curls of ivory napery were set on bone-white plates, and a centrepiece that combined a silver candelabra and scarlet hibiscus was the perfect complement.

By the time Matt opened the door into the adjoining sitting room Rachel was feeling dazed and definitely apprehensive. Surely anyone who lived in these surroundings had to be intimidating, and it was doubly disturbing when she felt she was here under false pretences.

There were three people in the huge sitting room. One, she saw at once, was Matt's sister Amalie, and the two older people were obviously his parents.

Despite the effort it evidently cost him, Jacob Brody got instantly to his feet. Leaning heavily on his walking stick, he would have started towards them if Matt hadn't stopped him.

'Hey, it's okay,' he said, leaving Rachel's side to go and help the older man back into his chair. 'Rachel will forgive you. Won't you, Rachel?'

Rachel made a helpless gesture. 'I—of course,' she said

quickly, and was aware of the older woman getting to her fe
also, and coming towards her.

'You must forgive Jacob, Rachel,' she said. 'He forge
he's not as agile as he used to be.' She smiled. 'I'm Diana,
the way. And that—' she indicated the girl still lounging
a huge red velvet sofa '—as I'm sure you know, is Amalie

'Yes.' Rachel allowed Diana to shake her hand in welcom
'We—er—we met in town the other day.'

'So I believe.' Diana's tone was dry, and Rachel wonder
what Amalie had told her mother about their encounter. 'L
me get you a drink.'

'I'll do that,' said Matt at once, reaching out a hand
beckon Rachel to join him. 'Come and meet my old ma
Rachel. He can't wait to introduce himself.'

'Not so much of the old,' retorted Jacob Brody staunch
his handshake unexpectedly firm. 'Take no notice of my so
Rachel. I admit I did want to meet you. Are you enjoying yo
stay on St Antoine?'

'Very much,' said Rachel, and at Jacob's suggestion sl
took the chair nearest to his. 'It's a beautiful island.'

'That is is,' agreed Jacob, with obvious satisfaction. 'O
family have lived here for almost two hundred years. N
always in such comfort, naturally.' He smiled and looked
at his son. 'Did you say something about getting Rache
drink?'

'Yeah, I did, didn't I?' Matt's smile was rueful. 'What c
I get you, Rachel? A glass of wine? Or perhaps you'd like
cocktail like Diana and Amalie are having.'

Diana?

Rachel frowned as she looked up at him, and she cou
tell by his lazily amused expression that he understood h
confusion 'Um—white wine, I think,' she said, aware she w
being overly cautious. But, heavens, did he call his moth
Diana? Or had she been misled? Wasn't Diana his moth
after all?

'Sure?'

His eyes were mocking her again, but she refused to be diverted. 'Yes, please,' she said firmly. 'Thank you.'

'So go and do your duty, Matt!' exclaimed his father impatiently, and Matt's mouth compressed in an effort to control his mirth.

'Oh, I intend to,' he said, his eyes on Rachel as he spoke, and she felt the hot colour rising up her throat. 'Excuse me for a moment, won't you?'

Despite herself, Rachel couldn't help watching him as he crossed the room to where a drinks cart had been installed. He took a bottle of white wine and another of beer from the chilled compartment, filling a glass for Rachel that seemed inordinately large.

'Have you seen much of the island?'

Jacob was speaking again, and Rachel forced her attention back to the man beside her. 'A little,' she said, biting her lower lip before continuing, 'I joined one of those picnic cruises this morning, and that was—that was—'

'Interesting?' suggested Matt, appearing beside her. He handed her the glass of wine, his amusement evident again. 'Unfortunately it didn't work out quite as well as she'd intended. She had to contend with—um—sunburn. Isn't that right, Rachel?'

Rachel's face was burning now. 'That's right,' she said tightly, knowing that Matt knew full well what she'd thought he'd been about to say. She straightened her spine as Matt propped his hip on the arm of her chair instead of seeking another. 'But yesterday your son was kind enough to—um—lend me some cream his grandmother used to use.'

Matt grinned, apparently enjoying her attempt to turn the tables. 'I think it's done some good. Don't you, Diana?'

Diana, who had returned to her seat beside her daughter on the sofa, nodded thoughtfully. 'Charley certainly knew a thing or two about herbal medicine,' she agreed. 'That's Grandma

Charlotte,' she explained for Rachel's benefit. 'I've used the cream myself on many occasions.'

Rachel smiled, trying to behave as if Matt's thigh wasn't wedged against her shoulder. He was holding his bottle of beer in one hand, but the other was hovering somewhere near the nape of her neck. Just occasionally a finger brushed her skin and she shivered. And, while her brain was warning her not to play his game, the temptation to reach up and cover his hand with hers was almost overwhelming.

She managed to resist, however, and thankfully the conversation became more general. Jacob wanted to know if Matt had had enquiries for any more charters, and Amalie grumbled that they weren't supposed to talk business when they had a guest.

Diana asked about her job in England. She seemed genuinely interested when Rachel explained she worked for a small local newspaper in Chingford.

'Jacob writes, too,' she said, drawing an impatient disclaimer from Matt's father. 'He does,' she insisted. 'He's researching a history of the island and the Brodys' part in it.' She chuckled. 'I've warned him he'll probably find out his ancestors were pirates or some such. No one on these islands can be absolutely sure their family wasn't involved in that or the slave trade.'

Rachel smiled. She liked Diana. The woman was doing her best to make her feel at home. Amalie, meanwhile, just sipped her cocktail, only making the most unenthusiastic attempt to air her views.

'Well, I think it's exciting,' Rachel said. 'My job just involves getting in touch with local businesses and asking them if they'd like to advertise in the paper. I've always envied people who have the talent to write.'

'That's a matter of opinion,' said Jacob drily, 'I'd much prefer to be out and about on my own again.'

'Oh, Jacob...'

Diana spoke sympathetically, and while his father was otherwise engaged Matt bent and put his lips close to Rachel's ear.

She sucked in a breath, aware of Amalie watching them and not sure what he was planning to do, but he only said softly, 'Pa had a stroke about three months ago. He's recovering well, but the doctors have warned him he can't go on doing as much as he did before.'

'Oh!'

Rachel pressed her fingers to her lips, her uneven breathing giving her away. Matt straightened, his eyes revealing he'd known exactly what she was thinking.

Trying to concentrate on other matters, Rachel acknowledged that, despite his evident weakness, Matt's father wasn't an old man. Evidently the stroke accounted for his use of a walking stick. But in spite of a small stoop he was still tall, like his son, and it must gall him to be confined to the house, however beautiful his surroundings.

'He'll be okay,' Matt added, as Diana turned back to address her daughter.

'Amalie, why don't you ask Rachel if she'd like another glass of wine?'

'Oh, no. Thank you.' Rachel spread her fingers over the rim of the glass that was still more than half full. 'I'm not much of a drinker, I'm afraid.'

'Everything in moderation,' murmured Matt teasingly, and Amalie gave her a sulky look.

'You should relax a little, Rachel,' she said, draining the dregs of her cocktail with a careless flourish. 'And don't let my brother fool you. He's not half as innocent as he seems.'

'Amalie!'

It was her father who spoke now, and the girl had the grace to colour slightly. 'Well,' she said defensively. 'We all know why he had to invite her here.'

'I invited her,' said Jacob coldly. 'And if you can't keep a

civil tongue in your head, young lady, you can spend the r
of the evening in your room.'

A sudden tap on the door was never more welcome, as
as Rachel was concerned. She had felt Matt tense beside I
and knew it was only a matter of time before he entered
exchange.

But Caleb's appearance diverted all of them. 'Dinne
ready when you are, Mr Jacob,' he said politely, and Ma
father pushed himself determinedly to his feet.

'Not a moment too soon,' he said, giving his daughte
final warning glance. He held out a hand to Rachel. 'Will y
give me your arm, my dear?'

'Of course.'

With a nervous look in Matt's direction, Rachel joined
father for the procession into the dining room. And she s
at once something she hadn't noticed earlier: only one end
the impressive table had been laid for dinner.

With Matt's assistance, Jacob was seated at the head of
table, with Diana and Rachel on one side and Matt and Ama
on the other. Rachel found herself talking mainly to Dia
the width of the table precluding any private conversat
with Matt.

The meal was delicious, but Rachel ate very little. A l
ster soufflé that melted in the mouth was followed by fres
caught grouper, a fish Rachel had never tasted before. Then
tenderest of fillet steaks with 'rice and peas', which was re
rice and red kidney beans, and a mix of exotic vegetables

By the time dessert came around Rachel had to refu
Although she'd only picked at her food, she knew she coul
eat another thing. She was sure the passionfruit mousse v
delectable, as Diana said, but all she wanted was coffe
finish the meal.

She noticed Matt hadn't shown much of an appetite eit
He spoke often with his father, and she guessed they w
talking business again. She encountered Amalie's eyes a ti

or two, quite by accident on her part, though probably not so on the girl's. That comment about Matt not being as innocent as he appeared still stuck in her mind.

'It's the only chance Jacob gets to find out what's going on in his absence,' murmured Diana in a low voice. 'He knows Matt is perfectly capable of running the company, but I'm afraid my husband is something of a work junkie.'

So Diana *was* Jacob's wife. 'Have you been married long?'

'Heavens, yes.' Diana spoke reminiscently. 'It's going to be thirty-five years in July. I can hardly believe it.' She grimaced. 'That's probably why Jacob used to spend so much time out of the house.'

Rachel smiled. 'My father's like that,' she said, feeling a renewed sense of guilt that she hadn't kept Ralph Claiborne informed of what she'd discovered. 'He enjoys his work, too.'

'What does he do?' asked Diana politely.

'Oh, he's an accountant,' replied Rachel, aware that Matt was also listening to their exchange. 'He was going to retire last year, but he changed his mind.' She paused then, and met Matt's considering gaze with one of her own. 'I think he wishes he had now.'

'Really? Why?'

Diana was interested, but Rachel was wishing she hadn't mentioned her father at all.

'Oh—just events,' she said offhandedly, accepting another cup of coffee from the maid who'd served their dinner. 'Thank you. This is delicious.'

'It's our own blend, you know.' To her relief, Jacob had heard what she'd said and now chose to enter their conversation. 'We cultivate it here at Jaracoba. Not an enormous amount, you understand, but enough for our own needs and the needs of most of the islanders.'

'Well, it's certainly good,' said Rachel admiringly. 'I'm ashamed to say I usually use instant at home.'

'Do you live with your parents?' asked Diana, and Rachel shook her head.

'No. I have a small apartment of my own.'

'Of your own?' Matt took her up on it. 'No partner?'

'No partner,' she said firmly, aware that she was blushing again. But, heavens, did he think she'd have allowed him to—well—touch her, if she'd been involved with someone else?

But perhaps he wasn't so discriminating…

The sound of a car racing up the drive carried on the still night air. An engine was revving far too noisily, tyres squealing, brakes screaming, as the vehicle was brought to a halt.

'What the devil—?' began Jacob irritably, half rising to his feet and then sinking back again when the door half opened and Caleb inserted his head into the space he'd created.

'You've got a visitor,' he was beginning, somewhat nervously, when the door was thrust open. Sara Claiborne, was just behind him, glaring over his shoulder, her eyes accusing as they swept round the table.

Rachel wanted to die. She felt sure her mother must have followed her here. Had she gone to the hotel and discovered her daughter had left with Matt Brody? Might they even have told her he was taking her to his home?

Whatever, surely Sara hadn't gone to the hotel dressed like that? Her scarlet catsuit clung to her generous curves; her stiletto heels were digging into the carpet.

She looked like a caricature of the woman Rachel had known all her life, and she couldn't understand what was going on.

'What do you want, Sara?'

It was Matt who spoke, pushing back his chair and regarding the visitor with a guarded gaze.

And Rachel realised she'd been wrong. Her mother hadn't come here to find her. It was Matt she wanted to see. Matt who, in spite of his obvious reluctance, brought a possessive smile to her face.

But then, as if remembering, her eyes moved back to Rachel again.

'What's *she* doing here?' she demanded, as if she had the right to do so. But now Jacob had had enough.

'I invited her,' he said. 'This is my home, and I'll invite who I like. I suggest you stop embarrassing yourself and Matt, Sara, and go back to Mango Key.'

CHAPTER ELEVEN

MATT drove Rachel back some thirty minutes later.

He was silent on the journey, and she couldn't exactly bla[me] him. It must have been embarrassing, having the two wom[en] he was involved with in the room together. It had been e[m]barrassing for her, goodness knew. And she'd done nothi[ng] wrong.

Yet.

But she refused to think about almost making love w[ith] Matt the evening before. She had to pretend that it had ne[ver] happened. And, let's face it, she reminded herself, nothi[ng] *had* happened.

Yet.

She shook her head, as if by doing so she could shake su[ch] thoughts away. But it wasn't easy. She was remembering t[hat] despite Jacob's words Sara hadn't agreed to leave until sh[e] had a private conversation with Matt. He'd escorted her [out] to her car, and in his absence conversation had stalled. Sar[a's] arrival had disturbed all of them, and only Amalie had seem[ed] to be enjoying the situation.

The return journey seemed to be over far too quickly. [In] spite of what had happened Rachel was sorry the evening h[ad] had to end like this. She'd been so full of anticipation at [the] start. But perhaps this was payback for thinking of no one b[ut] herself.

For once, Matt turned into the hotel forecourt. And inste[ad] of dropping her off at the entrance, as she'd expected, he parked the vehicle and got out. He'd circled the car and pulled open her door, too, before she'd had time to anticipate his actions. Then, helping her out, he said flatly, 'We need to talk.'

In spite of what she'd been thinking, Rachel knew that wasn't going to happen. Not tonight, anyway. Not while she was still distressed over what her mother had said.

'I—don't think so,' she said, turning towards the hotel entrance, but Matt's hand gripped her biceps.

'I do,' he said grimly. 'Come on. We'll go up to my suite.'

'Your suite?'

Rachel turned shocked eyes in his direction, and Matt gave her a weary look. 'You think I don't keep a suite of rooms at the hotel, just in case I need them?' he enquired drily. 'Sometimes it's not convenient to drive back to my house.'

Rachel shook her head. 'Even so...'

'Even so, nothing,' he said, turning her towards the entrance again. 'Come on. I'll buy you a drink before we go upstairs.'

'I—I don't want a drink,' stammered Rachel, even though the kick of alcohol might have been exactly what she needed.

'Not downstairs?' Matt chose to misunderstand her. 'Okay. I'll get one of the staff to bring a bottle to my rooms.'

'You don't understand—'

'No. *You* don't understand,' Matt interrupted her shortly, as they crossed the lobby. 'Wait here. I'll just speak to the barman about a bottle of wine.'

Rachel was almost to the top of the stairs when he caught up with her. She'd tried to hurry, but in her high heels it hadn't been easy. Matt was able to vault up two stairs at a time, and she had to concede there was no way she could get away from him in the hotel anyway.

When she would have turned towards her room, however, he stopped her. 'It's this way,' he said, and to her amazement, he directed her towards the double panelled doors which she knew led into the office. Of course the office would be empty at this time of day, but all the same...

Deciding she could hardly question his decision without provoking his curiosity, she shook herself free of his hand and walked beside him along the gallery. She realised they were in full view of anyone looking up from the foyer below, but she resigned herself to the knowledge that that was par for the course.

As expected, the office was deserted. Only dim security lighting illuminated desks and filing cabinets, the fax and printing machines she'd seen a few days ago. Surely Matt didn't intend that they should have a conversation here? He had mentioned a suite of rooms.

Matt closed the door behind them and then led the way across the room to where another door gave access to a narrow corridor. He switched on overhead lights and motioned for her to follow him. He then opened a door a few yards further on, and indicated that she should precede him into the room.

A switch at the door caused several lamps to spring to life, and Rachel saw at once that it was a small sitting room. Well, small by Jaracoba standards, she thought, her mind still filled with the magnificent dimensions of his home.

Twin leather sofas faced one another across a gleaming occasional table, their black surfaces highlighted by cushions in red and gold. There was a sound system and a large television; undrawn curtains hung at three long windows, matching the cushions in design.

Rachel was surprised by the beauty of the room. It was such an unexpected find beyond the commercial environs of the office. There were other doors that evidently gave access to a bathroom and a bedroom. Maybe even a kitchen, although she doubted Matt would bother making meals here.

Matt closed the door behind them and then leaned back against it. 'Sit down,' he said. 'The wine will arrive shortly.'

'I don't mind standing,' Rachel said, wandering across to the windows. But there was little to see beyond the panes but the floodlit grounds of the hotel.

Matt shrugged, and moments later there was a tentative knock at the door. He swung it open, then took the tray from the waiter with little ceremony, closing the door in the man's face with what Rachel recognised as barely controlled impatience.

It was only as he set the tray on the low table that she saw he'd ordered champagne. A bottle of Krug sat beside two crystal glasses, and, although she knew little about such things, she guessed only the best would do for him.

When he straightened again, and looked directly at her, Rachel shifted uneasily. His eyes were dark with anger and there was little compassion in his gaze.

'Come and sit down,' he said, and this time it sounded like an order. 'I have no intention of discussing anything with you hovering over there like Marley's ghost.'

Rachel squared her shoulders. 'Do we have anything to discuss?'

Matt's mouth twisted, and she saw the pulse beating at his temple. Oh, he was angry all right, she thought apprehensively. No wonder she was feeling so alarmed.

He blew out a breath, and for a moment she wondered if he intended to force her to obey him. But she should have known better. Instead, he bent and lifted the champagne, expertly easing out the cork and pouring himself a glass.

She was sure he drank it without tasting it. Which seemed his intention. He poured himself another and then looked at her again. 'You know,' he said, 'I can stay here all night if necessary.'

Rachel sighed. She was half wishing now that she'd not created this stand-off. He was right. It was silly. And counter-productive.

'All right,' she said, and with a little shrug she stepped

nervously towards him. 'I know you can always out-do me when it comes to an argument.' She paused beside one of the sofas, her nails digging into the soft leather. 'What did you want to talk about?'

Matt closed his eyes for a moment, as if he didn't quite believe her. Then, opening them again, he swallowed half the liquid in his glass before setting it back on the tray.

'Sit down,' he said, pointing to the sofa opposite him. 'Or do you want me to think you're scared of me? Believe me, you should be.'

Rachel remained where she was. 'Why don't you just tell me why you've brought me here?' she demanded. 'I assume you're feeling peeved about what happened. Well, don't think you can take your frustration out on me...'

'My frustration? My *frustration*?' The oath he uttered didn't bear repeating. 'You don't know anything about my frustration! If you did, you wouldn't stand there baiting me with stupid complaints.'

'You don't think I have room to complain?' she exclaimed, using anger to mask her apprehension. 'How do you think I felt when my mother walked into the room tonight?'

'How do I think *you* felt?' Matt was incredulous. 'How do you think *I* felt? My father can do without that kind of stress in his present condition.'

Rachel shook her head. 'I didn't invite her.'

Matt swore again. 'Do you think I did?'

'I don't know, do I?' she mumbled. 'Are you having an affair with her?'

'God, no.' He sounded appalled.

'But she came here to see you.'

Matt sighed then. 'That doesn't mean I'm having an affair with her, Rachel. Our relationship is nothing like that.'

Rachel wanted to ask what it *was* like, but she felt she'd gone as far as she could tonight. 'Anyway,' she said. 'It doesn't matter now. I'm tired. I want to go to bed.'

Matt stared at her, his green eyes as dark as laurel. His look was intent, dangerous, and despite everything Rachel couldn't look away.

'I want to go to bed, too,' he said, and now he moved, closing the space between them. His warm breath fanned her cheek and his quickened breathing matched her own.

Rachel would have backed away again, but his hand at her nape prevented her from moving at all.

'I want to go to bed with you,' he added, bending to brush the corner of her mouth with his lips. 'I want to make love with you and sleep with you and then make love with you again.'

Rachel's breath caught in the back of her throat. This was so much more than she had expected. He was so close she could feel the heat of his body enveloping her; so close she was suddenly aware of the pulse beating at the centre of her core.

Warm wet fluid drenched her panties and her limbs went totally weak. 'Matt—'

She tried to make a protest, but the truth was she didn't really want to stop him. She'd never felt a need like this before, never experienced such a craving that yearned to be fulfilled.

He moved even closer, taking the evening bag she was holding like a barrier in front of her and tossing it aside. Then he slipped an arm about her waist and pulled her against him, her breasts crushed against his chest, her hips against the hard muscles of his thighs.

'Sweet,' he said, his voice thickening with emotion, pushing a thigh between her quivering legs. 'Do you have any idea how much I want you?'

Then his mouth was on hers, hard and passionate. His tongue plunged between her teeth, exploring the moist cavity he found within. His tongue caressed hers, mated with hers, causing her to lean against him. And she heard his growl of appreciation when she allowed him to suck her tongue into his mouth.

She couldn't fail to be aware of his arousal, and her hands sought the waistband of his khakis for support. His hand cupped her chin, angled her face to please him, lengthening and deepening his kiss.

His free hand slid over her scalp. She felt the knot she'd made of her hair unravel, felt the weight of it loose about her shoulders.

'So beautiful,' he said, allowing the silky strands to slide through his fingers. Then he lowered his head and buried his face in its soft folds.

Blood was thundering through Rachel's veins like liquid fire. The increasing pressure of his erection against her stomach made her feel weak. He brushed a strand of hair from her cheek, and looked down at her with undisguised hunger.

'I've wanted you since that morning at Mango Cove,' he said huskily. 'Tell me you don't want me, too, and I'll let you go.'

Rachel shook her head. 'I—I can't,' she admitted. Her breathing was becoming more and more shallow, and he tipped back her head and trailed hot kisses down her throat.

'That's what I thought,' he breathed with evident satisfaction, his possessive touch making her feel as if she might swoon with pleasure.

A hot wave of desire was surging over her, making her body tremble, sweeping all her inhibitions away. She hadn't known it was possible to feel so out of control, yet so aware of what she was doing. Her body seemed to be working on instinct, knowing automatically what he wanted her to do.

When his mouth returned to hers again, her lips parted instinctively. She discovered his shirt had pulled free of his pants at the back, and her palms spread sensuously over hot male flesh. She'd never touched a man in this way before, never wanted the ultimate pleasure of exploring a man's body.

But she remembered how Matt had looked that day at the beach, and she wanted to see him that way again.

She was hardly aware that Matt had found the cords that tied the wraparound jersey about her. It was only when she felt the cool, air-conditioned draught on her shoulders that she realised her dress was down around her waist. And only there because of the closeness of their bodies. If Matt stepped away, it would tumble to the floor.

She was diverted by Matt's mouth caressing the upper slopes of her breasts. Her bra was still in place, but she knew it revealed as much as it concealed. She glanced down and saw her breasts were swollen, the nipples straining hard against the flimsy lace.

Matt cupped her breasts in his hands, and then startled her by bending to suckle her through her bra. The fabric got wet, but it was so sensual, so intimate. It added another feverish dimension to her need.

Then Matt unhooked the bra and discarded it. 'Let's find somewhere more comfortable,' he said huskily, and picked her up in his arms.

Rachel's head felt as if it was spinning. It was all happening too fast and she was so not ready for it. Nevertheless she wound her arms around his neck and pressed her face against his throat. Her cheek brushed against his chin, felt the roughness of his stubble. And the scent of his skin was so intoxicating that she forgot to be apprehensive.

Matt kicked open a door and she glimpsed the austerity of a dark carpet and the familiar dimensions of a huge bed. The light streaming in from the living room showed the silk spread that covered the bed. She felt its coolness against her bare back as Matt laid her on it. It reminded her that, although she was almost naked, Matt was still fully clothed.

An image she recalled from the previous evening.

She would have been happy to remain in semi-darkness, but Matt said, 'We need some light.' He turned on the lamp beside the bed and surveyed her with obvious satisfaction. 'I want to see you,' he said, peeling off his shirt with fingers that weren't quite steady. 'I want to see all of you.'

Rachel caught her breath when his hands went to his waistband. She wanted him naked, of course she did, but she couldn't help feeling nervous.

Then the bed depressed as Matt came to kneel beside her. 'You do it,' he said thickly, drawing her hands to the buckle of his belt.

Rachel took a gulp of air. She was trying to ground herself, but it wasn't working. Pushing herself into a sitting position, she prepared to do as he'd asked.

But her thighs parted automatically when she leaned forward, and Matt groaned and slipped his hand between her legs. He cupped her through her panties and his voice was hoarse with satisfaction when he said, 'You're wet.'

Rachel made a helpless gesture, not knowing how to react.

Matt had no such inhibitions. 'Incredible,' he continued, his finger invading the hem of her briefs and parting the tender lips of her womanhood. 'So ready,' he groaned, his voice rough with feeling as he found the already swollen nub at her core.

It was almost impossible to do anything while Matt was caressing her. The excitement building inside her was hastened by the erotic movements of his hand, and she wanted to part her legs wider, let him do whatever he wanted to prolong these amazing feelings. She gave a breathless little moan of anguish.

Somehow she managed to loosen his belt and unzip his khakis, though when his erection sprang into her hands she was understandably shaken. God, he was so big, she thought, her knowledge of a man's anatomy scanty at best. How could she want him so much and yet be so apprehensive?

Matt kicked off his shoes and his pants and then climbed

onto the bed beside her. He eased her back, and she relaxed again when he covered her mouth with his. Yet she couldn't stop herself from arching against him, from wanting more, much more, from him. Her hands sought him now, wanting to please him, and she was alarmed when he gave a muffled groan of protest.

'Easy,' he said against her mouth, nudging her thighs apart so he could lie between her legs. 'I'm only human,' he added ruefully. 'How much more of this do you think I can take?'

Rachel looked up at him, her eyes wide. 'A lot more, I hope,' she said impulsively, and then curled her legs around him when he buried his face between her breasts.

Once again she was conscious of the liquid pooling inside her. She could feel his erection pressing at the apex of her legs and she pressed herself against him, wanting him inside her. But instead he drew back, hooking his thumbs into the waistband of her panties and drawing them down her legs.

Then Matt was pressing his face against the damp curls he'd exposed. 'I—you can't do that!' she exclaimed, in a panic now. Her nails dug into his shoulders in protest at first, and then her hands sought his head, holding him closer.

'Better?' he asked, and all she could do was nod helplessly, lost in the needs he was inspiring.

Then his tongue probed between the curls and her body exploded. Waves and waves of pleasure tore through her, and despite her inexperience she knew what he'd done.

'But—I wanted *you*,' she whispered, and he trailed wet kisses across the slight mound of her stomach.

'And you'll have me,' he told her softly. 'I wanted to please you first.'

'You have,' she assured him as he worked his way up her body, nuzzling and kissing and biting her tender flesh. So much he'd rocked her whole world.

When he straddled her she tensed again, but only slightly. She was still experiencing the lingering rhythms of the pleasure he had given her, and even when he nudged her opening and eased a little way inside she wasn't alarmed.

'You're tight,' he said, but the way he said it she knew it wasn't a criticism. Then he cupped his hands beneath her bottom and lifted her to meet his urgent thrust.

He stifled the cry she uttered with his mouth, but he couldn't ignore the sudden obstruction that met his invasion. Yet he couldn't draw back. It was much too late for that. All he could do was bury himself inside her and then lift his head to stare down at her. The tears that had filled her eyes were a silent admission of what he'd done.

'Why didn't you tell me?' he demanded.

Rachel's tongue circled her lips. 'Does it matter?'

'Of course it matters,' he said. 'God, Rachel, you were a virgin. You should have told me.'

'I thought you wanted me,' she whispered.

'I did want you,' he retorted. 'God help me, I want you still. But it's wrong.'

'Is it wrong if I want you, too?' she protested. 'Please, Matt.' She felt his body stirring inside her and discovered she wanted more, needed more. 'Don't stop now.'

Matt gave a low groan that was half anguished, half humorous. 'I don't think I can stop,' he admitted harshly. 'But you've got to tell me if I hurt you again.'

Rachel nodded, slightly apprehensive again now, but she had no reason to be. Matt was so gentle at first, so controlled, that she felt her body relaxing until she felt his length filling her completely.

Then, as his own needs began to take over, her emotions quickened. He drew back, almost to the point of total withdrawal, before surging forward again. And as he did so her response became more demanding, and the feelings she'd had when Matt had seduced her with his tongue came back stronger than before.

There was no pain now. Her body was slick with moisture,

and Matt's movements created a wonderful friction that made what she'd felt before seem tame. This was real, this was urgent, this was making every nerve in her body react to his need. And the feelings just kept on building, until she felt as if all her senses had reached overload.

But then something magical happened. It was as if she'd been climbing a mountain and now she'd reached its highest pinnacle. With arms spread wide, she floated out over the precipice, her cry of fulfilment both mindless and sapped with pleasure...

CHAPTER TWELVE

MATT opened his eyes to find Rachel tiptoeing across the bedroom.

He must have fallen asleep, he realised, and with good reason. As well as making love a second time, which had been just as devastating as the first, they'd opened the champagne. He'd drunk several glasses of the intoxicating wine before exhaustion had obviously tugged him into oblivion.

But they had shared the most sensational sex he'd ever known. Somehow it had been more than just sex, he mused. It had been the closest thing to a spiritual experience he'd ever known. He'd never felt like this before. Never felt that instantaneous recognition of something stronger than himself.

'What are you doing?' he demanded now, propping himself up on his elbows. It was still dark outside, but there was a faint glow of sunrise on the horizon. The lamp beside the bed was still burning, however, and by its light he could see that Rachel had already found her panties and put them on.

'It's nearly morning,' Rachel whispered, and he noticed she had her arms crossed over her bosom.

He felt slightly irritated. Dammit, it wasn't as if he hadn't seen her breasts before. Seen them and kissed them and suckled from them, he remembered, his body stirring in spite of himself. God, he still wanted her. He had the uneasy feeling he was never going to have enough of her.

'It's still early,' he said, trying to keep his tone even. When what he really wanted to do was bound out of bed and carry her back into his lair. 'Come back to bed.'

'I don't want to be here when—when whoever occupies that office out there turns up for work,' Rachel declared, ignoring his suggestion. 'I'm sorry if I disturbed you. I didn't intend to.'

'So—what?' Matt stared at her, his mouth slightly belligerent. 'You were going to sneak out of here and hope I didn't hear you go?'

'It's not sneaking,' Rachel protested.

'What would you call it, then?' Matt scowled. 'Don't tell me you're regretting what happened last night?'

'Heavens, no.' Her response was so spontaneous he couldn't help but believe her. 'It's just—well—I can see you later, I suppose. After—after I've had a shower and dressed in some different clothes.'

'You could have a shower here.' Matt gestured towards the adjoining bathroom.

'No, thank you.' Rachel turned towards the door. 'I'll just go and find the rest of my things.'

'Let me,' said Matt, thrusting back the covers and getting out of bed. He wanted her to see his nakedness, to show he wasn't ashamed of himself, or her.

Rachel caught her breath at the sight of him. But at least it made her forget about covering herself as she opened the bedroom door.

Then he was behind her, drawing her back against his already aroused body. His shaft pulsed against her bottom, and she sucked in a little breath as his hands slid round to cover her breasts.

'Let me,' he said, bending his head to nibble on her shoulder. 'Don't go,' he added huskily. 'I want to make love with you again.'

Another indrawn breath proved she wasn't immune to his caresses. He felt her press herself against him almost involuntarily, and the feel of her soft bottom cradling his erection brought him close to losing control.

But, 'I'd better go,' she insisted, despite all reactions to the contrary. 'I mean it, Matt. I promise I'll see you later. I just need a little time to—to freshen up.'

He had to let her go. He had to watch as she picked up her bra and stuffed it into her handbag. Then she pulled on the wraparound gown she'd been wearing and hurriedly tied the cords. Without her bra, the dress was undeniably provocative, and with a muffled exclamation Matt said, 'Wait!'

This time she did wait, probably because she didn't want to spark his anger. There'd been sufficient irritation in his voice for her to realise he meant what he said. In a matter of minutes he'd hauled on his pants and thrown his shirt over his shoulders. 'I'll take you back to your room,' he said. 'We don't want anyone getting the wrong idea.'

He thought she wanted to argue, but perhaps she remembered Mark Douglas and changed her mind. 'Thank you,' she said, and, looking at her, he wondered if she really didn't regret what had happened.

She seemed so fragile, so remote; so much the innocent. He couldn't help but blame himself for taking advantage of her.

Rachel spent some time in the shower. It was good to feel the water sluicing all the perspiration from her skin. She felt tired—and a little sore—but otherwise wonderfully happy. It had been the most amazing night of her life and she couldn't wait to see Matt again.

She hadn't wanted to leave him that morning. She knew he had been concerned about her, and it would have been so easy to abandon any worries about what other people might think and crawl back into bed.

Into Matt's bed, she reminded herself with a little shiver

of excitement. Would he expect to sleep with her tonight? She really hoped so.

But then she remembered her mother.

She still had no doubt that Sara Claiborne had come to Jaracoba looking for Matt. He'd virtually admitted as much. But he'd also denied that he was having an affair with her.

So what did that mean? Had they had an affair in the past? Had her mother come here hoping to resurrect their relationship?

It was a situation Rachel didn't even want to consider, but she had to. Her father was in England, waiting for her to get back to him with some good news. But what could she tell him? That her mother had changed? That she was seriously thinking of staying on the island? That, whatever Matt said, Sara's association with him was anything but over?

She examined herself in the mirror when she came out of the shower cubicle. She didn't think she'd changed, outwardly at least. But she knew she was different inside. It wasn't so much a physical thing, although she knew that had changed too. But psychologically she was a different person.

There was another bite mark on her shoulder and she ran her fingers over it. And felt a tingling sensation right down to her toes. Her mouth was slightly swollen, but she wasn't really surprised. Matt's kisses had been full of raw passion.

However crazy she was, she couldn't wait to see him again. If she'd known the extension number of his apartment she might have called him. So it was probably just as well that she didn't. They had to talk again before anything more significant happened between them.

Although what could be more significant than last night's lovemaking?

Shaking her head, she grabbed a towel from the rack and quickly dried herself. Her hair was still damp when she fastened it back with a scrunchie, but she was too impatient to spend much time on it. Besides, her hands weren't quite steady, and she knew that whatever she did it would still persist in curling about her temples and her nape.

She dressed in lime-green shorts and a scoop-necked tee shirt which successfully hid the bite on her shoulder. She could do nothing about the mark on her neck, but the heat in her skin had faded and her incipient tan made it less conspicuous.

She used her mascara brush and an amber-coloured lip-gloss, slipped canvas flats onto her feet, and, after collecting her bag, left her room.

Her eyes were instinctively drawn to the double doors that led to both the office and Matt's apartment. But there was no sign of the hotel's owner, and, despite a sense of disappointment, Rachel descended the stairs.

Deciding that if Matt did come looking for her he would expect her to be on the patio, having breakfast, she crossed the foyer to the restaurant. A waiter seated her overlooking the pool, and she ordered coffee and French toast. For practically the first time since she'd come St Antoine she was hungry, and her lips twitched in rueful amusement. That was one outcome of losing her virginity that she hadn't anticipated.

She was just finishing her third cup of coffee when a flurry of movement caught her eye. She'd enjoyed the French toast, served with maple syrup, and despite a lingering sense of apprehension she was feeling pleasantly replete.

But the movement, accompanied by an impatient exchange with the waiter, drew her attention to the woman who was crossing the patio towards her.

Her mother.

Rachel caught her breath. She couldn't help it. She so didn't want to have a conversation with her mother. Not until she'd spoken to Matt again, anyway.

But that wasn't to be, and, putting down her cup, she got automatically to her feet. 'Hi, Mum.'

'I've told you not to call me Mum!' exclaimed Sara Claiborne angrily. Then, turning back to the waiter who had followed her, she added, 'Just fetch another pot of coffee. I don't want anything to eat.'

'Yes, ma'am.'

The waiter looked to Rachel, as if seeking her approval, and she nodded. What else could she do? This was her mother, after all. However outrageous she looked, still in the tight-fitting catsuit she'd worn the night before. Had she been to bed? Rachel didn't think so. And she suddenly wished she'd never had such a rich breakfast.

Sara pulled out a chair and sat down opposite her daughter. 'You're still here, then,' she said flatly. 'I thought I asked you to go back to London.'

Rachel sighed. 'You knew I was still here, Mum. You saw me at Matt's house last night.'

'I saw you at his *father's* house last night,' her mother corrected her. 'Matt doesn't live with his father. He has his own house. Where do you think I've been staying?'

'I see.'

It was a low blow, and Rachel did her best to hide her reaction.

'Oh, yes.' Sara knew her too well to be deceived by Rachel's attempt at indifference. 'It's a beautiful house. It overlooks the ocean. I'm very happy there.'

Rachel was sure she was. She just wished Matt had told her where her mother was staying. But then until last night they hadn't spoken about her mother at all.

'What do you want, Mum,' she asked now. 'Why have you come here?'

Sara gave her an incredulous look. 'What do I *want*?' she echoed. 'You know what I want, Rachel. I want you to go back to England and tell your father I'll be in touch with him when I'm ready, and not a moment before.'

Rachel gasped. 'Why don't you tell him yourself? There are such things as phones, you know. Even in paradise.'

Her mother's face contorted. 'Don't try to be clever with

me, Rachel. I know what you're doing. You and your father. You're trying to turn Matt and his family against me.'

'That's not true!' Rachel was appalled.

'It is true.' Sara spoke forcefully. 'And it's not going to work. They want me here. Matt wants me here. And I want to stay.'

Rachel couldn't believe her mother could be so obtuse. 'That wasn't the impression I got,' she murmured in a low voice. 'Please, Mum—'

'Don't call me that.'

'All right—Sara, then.' Rachel felt as if she was talking to a stranger. 'You know Dad loves you. I love you. Why don't you go home?'

Sara scowled. 'You see!' she exclaimed triumphantly. 'You *do* want to come between us.'

'Mum—Sara—Mr Brody didn't seem very pleased to see you last night. Surely—?'

'Jacob's just jealous, that's all.'

'Jealous!' Rachel wondered how much worse it could get. 'Mr Brody's not interested in you.'

'Did I say he was?'

Rachel was confused. 'You said he was jealous.'

'Yes. And he is. Jealous of my relationship with our son.'

Rachel felt sick now. 'Your—your son?' she whispered faintly.

'That's right.' Sara regarded her with suddenly critical eyes. 'Are you feeling all right? You've gone very pale suddenly.'

'I'm—I'm all right.'

Rachel didn't know how she got the words past the bile rising in her throat. But somehow she must not break down in front of this woman who had suddenly devastated her world.

'Well, if you're sure…'

'I'm sure.'

Rachel nodded, and her mother made an impatient little gesture as the waiter arrived with the coffee she'd ordered.

'Thank you,' she said shortly. And then, squaring her shoulders, she went on, 'You don't understand any of this, do you? I don't know what your father told you, but it obviously wasn't the truth.'

Rachel stared at her with disbelieving eyes. 'Does—does Dad know the truth?'

'About Matt? Of course he does.' Sara was dismissive. 'He's known for the last thirty-two years.'

Rachel couldn't speak. Nausea was rising in her throat now, and she was very much afraid she was going to throw up all over the breakfast table.

'I—excuse me,' she said abruptly, and, pushing up from the table, fled across the patio to the lobby and the public restrooms she'd seen there. She made it to the nearest cubicle with only seconds to spare. Her stomach heaved and she was violently sick.

She was still hanging over the bowl when she heard someone else come into the restroom. Praying it wasn't her mother, she remained silent, but Sara was no fool.

'Rachel?' she called. 'Is that you? What's wrong? What did your father tell you, for heaven's sake? Wait until I see him. I'll tell him exactly what I think of him, sending you out here to do his dirty work for him.'

Rachel sagged. She wanted to say her father hadn't sent her here for any underhand purpose, but that was no longer true. He'd known who Matt was when he'd sent her to find her mother. In God's name, why hadn't he told her the truth?

That Matt wasn't her mother's lover. He was Rachel's brother!

Rachel groaned and pulled a strip of toilet paper from the roll. Then she blew her nose. She was very near to tears, but she knew she had to behave as if it was her father who had upset her and no one else.

Flushing the toilet again, she unlocked the door and ope[n] it. She was sure she must look like death warmed over, a[nd] she could only hope that her mother would put her naus[ea] down to physical rather than emotional causes.

'What's wrong with you?' As Rachel went to wash h[er] hands at the basin her mother regarded her suspiciously. 'W[hat] did you have for dinner last night? Something's upset you a[nd] I can't believe it's anything I've said.'

Rachel had to suppress a gulp of anguish. How blind co[uld] her mother be? After everything that had been said, she s[till] had no conception of how her daughter was feeling.

'I—perhaps it was the French toast I had for breakfa[st,]' she mumbled. And then, realising her mother was quite [ca]pable of reporting this, she added, 'Or maybe it's just a c[hill] in my stomach. They say sunburn can do that. Chill you, y[ou] know.'

'Y-e-s.' Sara dragged the word out. 'Maybe.' She frown[ed.] 'Do you want to go back to the table?'

'Heavens, no!'

Rachel shook her head violently, and then wished she ha[d,] when the room swam around her. But her response had be[en] clear enough and her mother nodded.

'I suggest we go up to your room,' she said.

'I—my bag—'

'I'll get it.' For the first time Sara showed her a little c[on]sideration. 'What's the number of your room? I'll meet y[ou] there.'

The last thing Rachel wanted was for her mother to inva[de] the only private space she had. But, short of admitting th[at,] she had no choice. She gave her mother the number, and th[en] left the restroom to hurry up the stairs to her room.

Now she prayed she wouldn't see Matt. Dear God, s[he] hoped she never had to see him again…

CHAPTER THIRTEEN

RACHEL managed to get a seat on that evening's flight out of Jamaica.

The small inter-island plane that flew between St Antoine and Montego Bay connected with the large jet that would transport her to London, and Rachel had been relieved to find she had to leave for the airport before noon.

Sara Claiborne had been quite happy to use her local knowledge to get her daughter on board the propeller-driven aircraft, obviously as eager as Rachel was to get her off the island.

Rachel knew her mother thought she was leaving because she'd found out that her father's reason for sending her here had been a lie. The idea that her daughter's relationship with Matt might have something to do with her desire to leave didn't seem to occur to her. She didn't even question the fact that Rachel seemed in no hurry to get know her new brother.

Rachel shuddered at the thought. Thank God Matt had evidently had other matters to attend to that morning. By the time he realised she was gone she'd be off the island.

Yet, for all that, the day had dragged. Rachel didn't honestly know how she got through it. Allowing Sara into her bedroom, the room where she and Matt had first acknowledged their attraction to one another, had been harrowing, and pretending that the reason her stomach was upset was due to a chill, had torn her apart.

What she'd really wanted to do was lock herself away somewhere and cry like a baby. She was desolate, devastated, and no one—particularly not her mother—could comfort her.

Fortunately, Sara had been too wrapped up in her own affairs to notice her daughter's condition. And it had soon become obvious from her conversation that she was jealous of anyone who spent any time with her son.

She hadn't explained how Matt had come to be living with his father. All she'd said was that she'd made a terrible mistake in giving him up. She'd glossed over the details of her son's birth, giving the impression that the Brodys were to blame for what had happened.

In all honesty Rachel had hardly listened to her. She didn't want to hear that Jacob Brody had seduced her mother and then gone ahead and married someone else. Diana, she assumed. The whole situation was anathema to her, and she just wanted to put the whole damning episode behind her.

She didn't really relax until the big jet lifted off from the airport at Montego Bay. There'd been a two-hour delay between planes, and she'd been terrified Matt might discover what she'd done and come after her.

But no one came after her; no one spoke to her. She'd sat in the comfortable Club lounge and her attitude had evidently deterred any would-be acquaintance from approaching her.

The plane was due to land at Heathrow soon after eight o'clock the next morning, and although she would have preferred to make her own way home Rachel felt obliged to give her father the chance to meet her, if he wanted to.

She phoned him a couple of hours before they were due to land. And, even taking into account that she'd got him out of bed, Ralph Claiborne was shocked to hear from her.

'Why didn't you phone me before you left?' he demanded. 'Have you seen your mother? I must say I've been expecting you to ring for days.'

Rachel didn't want to get into that on the phone, particularly not on the plane, with half a dozen waking passengers more than interested to hear what she was saying.

'I'll tell you all about it when I see you,' she said. 'Don't worry about it. I can get a taxi home.'

'I wouldn't dream of letting you wait for a taxi,' he exclaimed. She could imagine him checking the clock as he spoke. 'You're due to land in a couple of hours, you say? That should give me time to get there.'

'Dad, it's the rush hour.'

'Don't be silly. I know a few short-cuts. I'll be there.'

Rachel shook her head. 'Okay.'

'Love you,' he said in farewell, but Rachel couldn't answer him.

Ignoring her fellow passengers, she folded the phone, drew her legs up to her chest and rested her chin on her knees. It was still dark outside the plane, dark and lonely, and for the first time since leaving St Antoine she allowed herself to think about Matt.

What was he thinking? she wondered. He must have discovered she'd left the island by now. Not that it would be any surprise to him, she thought painfully. If her mother had told him what she'd told her daughter, he would know how devastated Rachel must feel.

She didn't want to think about Matt's part in this, but it was difficult to avoid it. Hadn't it bothered him at *all* that their relationship was taboo? Or, like her, had he felt that irresistible compulsion? A compulsion that she now knew was forbidden.

A choking sob rose in her throat.

Oh, God, how could she bear it? Just twenty-four hours ago they'd been together. Twenty-four hours ago she'd been happier than she'd ever been in her life before.

Wrapping her arms around herself, she felt the hot tears welling in her eyes, spilling over. Tears streamed down her cheeks, dripping onto her arms, salty rivulets trickling into her mouth. She would never get over this, never. In just a few short days he'd turned her world around. He meant so much to her now. She cared about him. She *loved* him.

And it was so wrong.

Oh, God!

'Are you all right, Ms Claiborne?' One of the cabin staff had noticed her distress and was now hovering over her, blocking her from public view.

Rachel sniffed, trying to pull herself together. She had a tissue in the pocket of her jeans and she struggled to get it out. It tore as she did so, and she smeared a hand across her burning face.

'Sorry,' she mumbled, realising she was hardly an advertisement for the airline. 'I'm just feeling a bit emotional, that's all.' She sniffed again. 'Family problems, you know?'

The girl frowned and handed her a handful of tissues taken from the drinks trolley. 'Are you sure?'

'Oh, yes.' Rachel thanked her for the tissues and used them to dry her eyes. 'Have we much further to go?'

'Just over an hour.' The girl hesitated. 'Can I get you something to drink? A vodka and tonic, perhaps?'

Rachel managed a faint smile. 'At six o'clock in the morning?' she said humorously. 'I don't think so.'

'Well, if you change your mind...'

'Thanks.' Rachel sniffed again. 'I appreciate your concern.'

And she did. In a few words the attendant had shown her more sympathy than her mother. It hadn't even occurred to Sara Claiborne to question whether Rachel was fit to travel over four thousand miles when she'd been so sick.

But that was okay. Rachel reminded herself firmly. Her mother's sympathy was something she could do without.

It was a quarter to nine by the time she cleared passport control and collected her luggage from the carousel. But Ralph Claiborne was waiting patiently just outside Customs, and,

despite the feeling of betrayal she still felt, Rachel didn't hesitate before going into his arms. The real reason he'd sent her
to St Antoine, the lies he'd told her about her mother, mattered
less at that moment than the exquisite sense of security she
felt when his familiar arms closed about her.

She couldn't help herself then. She started crying again,
and her father drew back in some alarm, gazing at her with
anxious eyes. 'Rachel?' he said questioningly, but she just
shook her head.

'Not now, Dad,' she said, and although she knew he would
have liked an explanation he seemed to realise she was on the
edge of a complete breakdown.

A couple of hours later, at her parents' apartment, with the
cup of filtered coffee her father had made in her hand, Rachel
knew she couldn't prevaricate any longer.

'Why didn't you tell me you knew who Matt Brody really
was?' she asked, controlling the urge to rail at him. 'You let
me think Mum was having an affair with him.'

'I know.' Ralph Claiborne didn't try to deny it. He seated
himself opposite her at the kitchen table. 'But if I'd told you it
was Jacob Brody I was worried about, I'd have had to explain
who Matthew Brody was.'

Rachel blinked. 'And that would have been a problem?
How?'

'Oh, Rachel, haven't you realised yet? That wasn't my secret
to tell.'

'So you admit it was a secret?'

'Your mother's secret, yes.'

Rachel shook her head. 'And what do you mean, you were
worried about Mum and Jacob Brody? Matt's father's happily
married.'

'Is he?'

'Yes.'

'You've met him?'

'Yes.'

'But I understand he had a stroke a couple of months ago?'

'He did, yes.' Rachel was confused. 'What does that have to do with anything?'

Her father sighed. 'You'll have realised that he and your mother knew one another many years ago?'

'Well, she didn't tell me, but yes,' said Rachel heavily. 'So?'

'Oh, Rachel, I shouldn't be telling you this. She should.'

'But she's not here, is she?' said Rachel, struggling to keep her own feelings at bay. 'Please, Dad, I need to know. Why was I never told there was someone else before you? That she had another child?'

Ralph rested an elbow on the table and cupped his chin in his hand. 'Because—well, because from what I've gathered over the years it wasn't like that.'

'*What* wasn't like that?' Rachel was confused.

'Let me start at the beginning.' Her father took a steadying breath. 'First of all, when I got to know your mother, she told me that she'd had a baby. She knew we were getting serious about one another, and she wanted there to be no secrets between us.'

Rachel stared at him. 'So how young was she when she had—the baby?'

'Sixteen.'

'Sixteen!' Rachel was incredulous.

'Yes, sixteen. She and her parents had taken a holiday on St Antoine, and during the course of their stay she got to know Jacob Brody.'

He paused again, and then continued, 'I believe he was a few years older than she was—twenty, or thereabouts. But your mother was quite open about the way she'd pursued him. And over the two weeks she'd allowed him to—well—'

'I get the picture,' said Rachel tersely. 'Go on.'

'Of course when she got back home and found she was pregnant she was terrified. Things were very different in those days, and there was no question of her becoming a single mother. As I understand it, her father wrote to Jacob's father and told him of the situation. And in a matter of weeks it was decided that when the baby was born Jacob Brody would become its legal guardian.'

So that was what Matt had meant when he'd told her he'd been born in England, but had lived all his life on the island.

'You and Mum got married when she was nineteen, didn't you?'

'That's right.' Her father nodded. 'And to begin with we were very happy.'

'But?'

He sighed. 'I suppose you were about thirteen years old when she told me she'd kept track of Matthew's life for the past eighteen years. I thought at first she'd kept in touch with Jacob Brody, but after what you've just told me I doubt it. But somehow, maybe via a third party, she'd learned that Matthew was going to go to Princeton University that autumn. She told me she wanted to get in touch with him, to go and see him, to try and mend the rift between them.'

'Oh, Dad!'

'Yes.' He sounded weary now. 'It was a shock. I don't deny it. Her own parents were dead by that time. You remember they were killed in that train accident when you were twelve years old? Maybe she'd been thinking about it since then. I don't think Sara would have done anything against her parents' wishes, but after they were dead...'

'So did she go?'

'Oh, yes. According to her, Matthew was delighted to see her. Somehow I doubt that, too, but anyway, he didn't turn her away. I know Jacob Brody wasn't too happy about the arrangement. He and his wife regarded themselves as Matthew's parents. There was an exchange of letters in which he voiced his disapproval. But Matthew was above the age of consent, and I'm sure your mother had taken that into consideration when she made her move.'

Rachel was appalled. 'And has she seen him since then?'

'A couple of times,' agreed her father flatly. 'You remember that trip to Paris she made with your aunt Laura? That was to see Matthew. Then once she flew out to Miami and met him there.'

'But not to St Antoine?'

'Not until now.' Ralph Claiborne sighed again. 'That's what worried me so much. She'd heard that Matthew's father had had a heart attack or a stroke, or some such thing, and she told me she wanted to be with Matthew, to comfort him at this time.'

'But you didn't believe her.'

'No.' Her father was honest. 'Rachel, Jacob Brody is her son's father! No one has a stronger hold on her affections than him.'

Rachel was bewildered. 'But you're *my* father.' She thought she might cry again. 'Don't I mean anything to her at all?'

'Oh, Rachel, of course you do.' Ralph leaned across the table and covered her hand with both of his. 'We both love you very much. You know that.'

'But a son means so much more. Is that it?'

'No.' Her father was looking worried again now. 'Oh, Rachel, dear, don't press me. Your mother has her own way of doing things, as you should know. She'd never forgive me if I started rocking the boat now.'

Rachel couldn't believe it. Pushing herself up from the table, she said, 'Don't you think she's the one who's rocking the boat, Dad?' She gazed at him despairingly. 'She's talking about staying on the island. She says she wants to be with Matt. What else does she have to do before you realise we come a very low second on her list?'

Ralph gazed up at her with anxious eyes. 'She said that? She said she wants to stay on St Antoine?'

'Well...' Rachel had to be completely honest. 'She said she was happy there. She didn't say she wasn't coming back, but she didn't say she was either.'

'Damn her!'

It was the first time she'd heard her father swear in connection with her mother. She knew they'd had arguments from time to time, but her father had always moderated his language in her presence. Now, however, he seemed almost desperate in his need to voice his feelings. Rachel felt guilty for being the one to burst whatever bubble he'd been living in, but he had to know what her mother was thinking. He had to know there was a chance she might not come back.

A sudden knock at the kitchen door had them both lifting their heads in surprise. 'It's only me, Ralph,' called a light feminine voice, and Rachel's aunt Laura opened the door and came confidently into the room.

'Oh, Rachel!' she exclaimed when she saw her niece, and Rachel guessed she was the last person Laura had expected to see. 'I didn't know you were due back today.'

'She wasn't,' said Ralph heavily. 'Apparently your sister is considering staying in St Antoine, so Rachel decided to come home.'

That wasn't quite how it had been, but Rachel was happy to allow him that concession at least.

Laura gasped, however. She was a pretty woman, a few years younger than her sister, and plumper. 'You're not serious?' she exclaimed. 'Oh, that silly woman! I mean—'

She broke off abruptly, looking to Ralph as if for guidance, and her brother-in-law ran a heavy hand down his face. 'Rachel knows about Matthew,' he said. 'Sara's told her.'

'Oh...' Laura appeared relieved. 'Well, anyway, Matthew's what? Thirty-five? Thirty-six? He won't want his mother on his back for the rest of his life.'

'Tell me about it.' Ralph got to his feet and lifted his shoulders in a weary gesture. Then, forcing his thoughts into other

channels, he nodded his head towards the dish she was hol
ing. 'What's that you've got there?'

'Oh, it's just a casserole I made for your supper,' said Lau
deprecatingly, looking apologetically at Rachel. Then, as
some explanation was necessary, she continued, 'Your fath
gave me a key so I could get in and tidy the place while I
was at work. Obviously I didn't expect him to be home th
morning. Or you either,' she added. She forced a smile. 'D
you have a good trip? Or is that a silly question?'

'It's a silly question,' grunted Ralph.

Rachel, who was beginning to feel like a third wheel, sai
'I'll just use the bathroom, Dad. Then I'll go back to m
apartment. I dare say I've got some tidying up to do before
go back to work.'

'You could stay here,' suggested her father, but Rach
shook her head.

'No, I couldn't.' She smiled at Laura. 'Excuse me.'

Her father patted her shoulder as she passed him, b
Rachel didn't have the strength to return the gesture. It hu
a little to know that even her aunt had known about Matt
existence, but obviously she would. When Sara had been pu
suing Jacob, Laura wouldn't even have reached her teens. B
she'd definitely have been old enough to know her sister w
pregnant.

She went into the bathroom that adjoined her parent
bedroom. She wasn't surprised to see how pale she was. Sh
was surprised her aunt hadn't commented on it. But the
she suspected Laura had had enough to do, making excus
for running after her father while her mother was away. Sa
needed to get home soon, before her sister took over her hu
band as well as her home.

The urge to cry again swept over her, and she stifled
groan. Dear heaven, she felt as if her whole metabolism w
breaking down. She never cried; not normally. But then aga
these were hardly normal times.

She was walking back along the hall again when she heard her name mentioned. Not by her father, this time, but by her aunt.

'You didn't tell Rachel the truth?' she was saying, her voice full of impatience. 'Oh, Ralph, the girl's thirty, for goodness' sake! I don't care what Sara thinks. She deserves to know!'

CHAPTER FOURTEEN

DON GRAHAM stopped by Rachel's desk on his way back to his office.

'Rachel,' he said, and for once there was no trace of censure in his tone—which hadn't been the case for the past three weeks.

Since her return to work, he'd seemed to be constantly on her case, and she couldn't exactly blame him. Her concentration was spotty, at best, and she knew her work was suffering.

But what could she do? Her whole world seemed to have tilted on its axis, and although the relief of learning that Matt wasn't her brother was paramount in her thoughts, the knowledge that he'd known the truth all along put an entirely different complexion on their relationship.

Which was good—and bad.

Thanks to Aunt Laura's intervention, she now knew that she'd been adopted by the Claibornes when she was only a few days old. Her biological mother had been a law student, who'd had no intention of keeping the baby in any case, but who had died from a blood infection soon after the birth. She'd been unmarried, and no one seemed to know who Rachel's father had been. Another student seemed the most likely solution.

Sara's reasons for keeping this from her daughter seemed selfish, in retrospect, but Rachel wasn't into judging anyone. It had been common enough in the past for parents to keep their child's adopted status a secret, and after what Sara must have suffered when her son was taken from her there was some justification for her decision.

After the first initial shock Rachel had been prepared to be generous. She believed her father when he said he would have told her sooner, and, after all, he'd suffered enough in his own way.

Not that he seemed to be suffering now, she acknowledged. Aunt Laura was making herself a very satisfactory substitute so far as a housekeeper was concerned. It was to be hoped her mother knew what she was doing, Rachel mused ruefully. Laura might just try to dislodge her sister in a far more intimate way.

And as for Matt...

Well, if it hadn't been for Matt there wouldn't have been this dilemma. For her, or her mother.

But Matt was a factor. Rachel knew in her heart of hearts that if she'd known the truth she'd never have left the island as she had. And it would be so easy to blame Sara for that, too.

God knew what he must think of her. Would her mother have explained that so far as Rachel had been aware he was her brother? Or would that have been too much like admitting defeat? And, in any case, Sara had no idea how far their relationship had gone.

So far as Matt as concerned Rachel had left without even saying goodbye. And after what they'd shared that must seem the deepest cut of all.

Or perhaps not. She didn't know how Matt felt about her. Yes, he'd been attracted to her. Yes, he'd made love to her. But he must have made love to dozens of women, and surely if he'd really cared about her he'd have come after her. Just because she'd instinctively known that he was going to be the love of her life it did not mean that he felt the same. Obviously he didn't.

'Rachel?'

Don Graham was still standing beside her desk, and Rac[hel] realised that once again her thoughts had been wandering

Colour stained her cheeks. 'I'm sorry.' She pushed b[ack] her chair and got awkwardly to her feet. 'Did you want [me] Don?'

The possibility that he was thinking of dismissing [her] crossed her mind. And who could blame him? Her work d[efi]nitely wasn't up to standard. She hadn't signed up any [new] accounts for the past three weeks.

'You've got a visitor,' he said in a calming voice. 'It's y[our] mother.'

Rachel stared at him in disbelief. She and her father [had] been getting used to the fact that Sara Claiborne would ret[urn] home when she was ready and not before. And her fat[her] had said nothing about her mother coming home when sh[e] phoned him the night before.

'Yes, your mother,' said Don Graham kindly, squeez[ing] her arm. 'Look, your dad's told me she's been staying w[ith] friends, and that there's been something of an upset in [the] family. But she's here now, and she seems eager to spea[k to] you.'

Rachel swallowed, glancing across the office to whe[re a] wall of frosted glass hid the reception area. Her mother [was] here? At the *Chingford Herald*? To see her? Why?

'I've told Valerie to put her in the interview room,' w[ent] on Don Graham evenly. 'I'm sure you have lots to talk ab[out] so I'm giving you the rest of the day off. It's Friday. I'll [see] you again on Monday. Okay?'

Rachel was tempted to say no, it wasn't okay. Why sho[uld] she be available when her mother wanted her, when for [the] past few weeks she hadn't heard a word from her?

But she wasn't that kind of person. Whatever her mot[her] wanted, whatever reason her father had had for keeping [her] return a secret, she had to deal with it.

'Okay,' she said in a low voice, aware that once again she was attracting attention from the people around her. 'Thank you.'

Don Graham merely arched his brows and walked away, and, feeling much like a condemned woman on her way to the scaffold, Rachel walked slowly towards the office door.

Sara Claiborne was seated at the table in the interview room. Someone, probably Valerie, had supplied her with a mug of coffee, but she had barely touched it. And as soon as she saw her daughter she rose immediately to her feet.

'Oh, Rachel,' she said, and there was a break in her voice. 'I've been such a fool!'

Rachel closed the door behind her and leaned back against it. Despite fair warning, she found that seeing her mother again had made her legs feel decidedly wobbly. And, although she was sure Sara would have appreciated a hug, too much had happened to allow her to expose her emotions once again.

Squaring her shoulders, she said instead, 'Dad didn't tell me you were back.'

'That's because your father doesn't know yet,' said her mother heavily. 'I just flew in this morning and came straight here. I guessed you'd be at work and I needed to speak to you.' She paused. 'Alone.'

Rachel pushed away from the door. 'Well, don't you think you ought to ring Dad first? He's been really worried about you.'

'I'm sure your aunt Laura's been looking after him,' said Sara, somewhat cynically.

'Well, you can't blame Dad for that.'

Sara sighed. 'I'm not blaming anyone, Rachel. Except perhaps myself.' She spread an arm. 'Look, can we go somewhere we can have a private conversation? I never trust newspaper offices. They have microphones everywhere.'

Rachel shook her head. 'How about McMillan Court?' she

asked, naming the complex where her parents' apartment w
situated. 'It's private there.'

Her mother hesitated. 'Couldn't we go to your apartme
Rachel? I don't want us to be interrupted.'

Rachel bit her lip. It was true that although her father wou
be at work Aunt Laura had a key, and might well be doin
little housework in his absence.

'All right,' she said at last. She glanced at her watc
'There's a bus in fifteen minutes.'

'We'll get a cab,' said Sara firmly, bending to pick up h
handbag, and Rachel suddenly noticed the suitcase standi
behind the door.

'Okay,' she said, reaching for the handle of the case. 'I
just get my things.'

Traffic being what it was, it took them almost an hour
reach Rachel's apartment. An older complex than the o
where her parents lived, it was nevertheless equipped wi
all the usual amenities. A lift transported them to the seven
floor, and Rachel opened the door to number 702.

Not surprisingly, perhaps, her mother had said little in t
taxi. There was a definite rift between them, and althou
they'd spoken about the weather, and the contrast betwe
the chilly March day outside the windows and the heat of
Antoine, they were casual comments that anyone might ha
made.

Once they stepped inside Rachel's apartment, howeve
she heard her mother breathe a sigh of relief before collap
ing somewhat ungracefully onto the sofa in the living roor
Sara leaned back and closed her eyes, and for the first tin
Rachel allowed herself to notice that the years her mother h
appeared to shed in St Antoine had returned, with interest

Grey streaks were appearing in her hair again, and benea
her fur-lined jacket her flared woollen trousers and crev
necked sweater were anything but flamboyant. She look

pale, and tired, and when she opened her eyes again Rachel was amazed to see they were filled with tears.

'Oh, Mum,' she exclaimed, starting towards her, sympathy for the woman who'd raised her overcoming any resentment she'd been feeling. But her mother's next words halted her in her tracks.

'Matt and I have had such a terrible row,' she said brokenly, tears starting to trickle down her cheeks. She sniffed noisily. 'He hates me. I know he does. Oh, Rachel, why did you ever go to St Antoine?'

Rachel sat down rather abruptly on the arm of the nearest chair. 'Why did I ever go to St Antoine?' she echoed faintly. 'You know why I went, Mum. I was looking for you.'

'Oh, I know that.' Sara was testy. Sitting up, she reached into her handbag for a tissue. 'I know why you went there, you silly girl. I want to know what you think it had to do with you?'

Rachel's jaw sagged. 'Mum—Dad was worried about you. I was worried about you. We didn't know what to think.'

'Your father thought I'd gone there to see Jacob, didn't he?' Sara spoke impatiently. 'As if I would. But he had no right to send you there, involving you in my affairs.'

Rachel straightened her spine. 'So why don't you take this up with Dad?' Any sympathy she'd been feeling had quickly fled. 'I can't imagine why you would come here to talk to me.'

'Can't you? *Can't you?*' Her mother stared at her. 'Didn't you hear what I said? Matt and I have had a terrible row.' She swallowed convulsively. 'About you!'

'Me?' Rachel was glad she was sitting down at that moment. She didn't think her legs would have supported her. But she had to ask the obvious question. 'Why?'

'Oh, don't be coy.' Sara was contemptuous. 'I know what's been going on—don't you understand? Between you and Matt.' She paused. 'He told me.'

Rachel didn't know what to think. She couldn't think o
any occasion when she might have come under discussion
between Matt and her mother.

Unless…

'Well?' Sara was waiting for her to speak. 'Don't you have
anything to say for yourself?' She shook her head. 'I must say
when he first told me I could hardly believe it.'

Rachel stiffened. 'Why? Because you don't think I'm goo
enough for him?'

'Oh, don't be so silly.' Her mother wasn't having that. 'No
No. It's just you've always been such a—such a—'

'Recluse?'

'No.' Sara sighed. 'But you've always kept men at a dis
tance.'

Rachel shrugged. There was nothing to say to that.

'I can only assume that you allowed the island—and Matt
of course—to go to your head.'

Rachel's lips twisted. 'Something like that.'

Sara shook her head. 'It didn't bother you that to all intent
and purposes he was your brother?'

'How dare you say that?' Rachel was horrified. 'My God
I didn't even know he was your son. I thought you and he
were—were—'

'No!' Sara stared up at her, aghast. 'You can't have though
that a man like Matt would be interested in someone of my
age.' Her lips curled. 'He barely acknowledges me as hi
mother.'

'Whose fault is that?' Rachel knew her words were hurtful
but her mother had hurt her, too. 'I think you'd better go.'

'Not yet.' Sara got to her feet. 'There's something you nee
to know.'

'What?' Rachel was contemptuous now. 'If you're going
to tell me that I was adopted, don't bother. I already know.'

'You know?' Evidently this was what Sara had intended

to say. Rachel wondered why she'd suddenly decided to tell her the truth. After all these years, it was incredible.

'How did you find out?'

Rachel shrugged. 'I heard Dad and Aunt Laura talking. Does it matter? I know now. You can save your confession for someone else.'

Sara caught her breath. 'Don't be cruel, Rachel. You don't know what I've had to suffer all these years. But I might have known Laura wouldn't be able to keep her mouth shut. She's never understood what it's been like for me.'

'And what about Dad?' demanded Rachel. 'Don't you think he's suffered, too?'

'But Matt's my son, Rachel.'

'And you've never let Dad forget it, have you?'

Sara bent her head. 'I thought I'd have other children,' she said. 'I wanted at least three. But—well—we discovered your father had a problem. That was why I agreed to an adoption.'

'And you got me,' said Rachel bitterly. 'How disappointing for you.'

'Oh, don't say that.' Her mother heaved a sigh. 'Look, Rachel, I know we've never been as close as a mother and daughter should be, but I loved you. I *love* you. You must know that.'

'But not as much as you love Matt,' said Rachel sadly. 'I really think you'd better go, Mum. Just pray Dad has more sympathy for you than I do right now.'

'702 Lincoln Place.'

Matt murmured the words in an undertone as he stood looking up at the tall apartment building.

So this was where Rachel lived, he mused, trying to suppress the sense of trepidation he felt at invading her space without an invitation. What if he'd been mistaken? What if she really didn't want to see him again? At barely eight o'clock on a Saturday morning she probably wasn't even awake, let alone up and dressed.

Still, he hadn't flown all this way just to turn back at the first obstacle. He had to see her; he needed to see her. He had to know what his mother had said to her. Dear God, had she really let the girl go on thinking she was his sister?

He hadn't found out that Rachel didn't know she was adopted until Thursday evening. He'd always known Sara had an adopted daughter. She'd made a point of telling him that she wasn't Rachel's biological mother.

He'd naturally assumed she'd told Rachel the same. Discovering that she hadn't had put a whole new slant on Rachel's reasons for leaving, and he'd wanted to strangle his mother for causing such a tangled skein of grief.

God, how could she do it? Knowing he was attracted to Rachel? Was that why? Was she so jealous of anyone who got close to him that she'd go to any lengths to protect herself?

He'd been shattered when he'd found out Rachel had left the island, and his mother had known that. But she hadn't said a word about speaking to her daughter before she left.

Naturally he'd blamed himself. He'd been sure Rachel must have had second thoughts. She'd seemed so fragile, so vulnerable; a virgin, for heaven's sake. And he'd plunged into a full-blown affair. He'd convinced himself that she hadn't been prepared to continue their relationship on those terms and for the past three weeks he'd buried his misery in work.

Then, on Thursday evening, he'd had dinner with his father. Diana had been attending a meeting of her music festival committee, and Amalie had been out with her boyfriend. So there had been just the two of them.

Jacob was getting stronger every day, but to Matt's surprise seemed quite content with the way his son was handling the business.

'I'm beginning to enjoy researching my book,' he'd confessed ruefully. 'Perhaps I'm getting lazy in my old age. All I need now is an assistant to translate my notes into some kind of coherent language.'

Matt smiled, but he wasn't really in the mood to discuss his father's occupation. He was finding it harder every day to conduct even a civil conversation with his employees, and this taciturnity did not go unremarked.

'Sara still giving you a hard time?' asked his father understandingly. 'When is that woman going to go home?'

'God knows.' Matt pushed his steak aside and lay back in his chair. 'I think she believes I want her here. But she couldn't be more wrong.'

'It's a pity Rachel couldn't stay longer,' remarked Jacob thoughtfully. 'You and she seemed to get along so well. She's a lovely girl.'

Matt's lips tightened. 'Yes, she is.'

'It's a shame that you and she are related. In other circumstances—'

'Related?' Matt stared at his father.

'Well, you do have the same mother,' Jacob pointed out mildly. 'I mean—'

'We don't have the same mother,' Matt interrupted him sharply. 'Why would you say a thing like that? You *know* Rachel was adopted by the Claibornes.'

Jacob's jaw dropped. 'No, I didn't know that.' He shook his head. 'How could I? You and I hardly talk about your mother, goodness knows, let alone her daughter.'

'But—' Matt straightened in his chair. 'Sara must have mentioned it.'

'No. No, she hasn't.' Jacob was very definite about that. 'It's not the sort of thing she would tell me, now, is it?'

'My God!' Matt pushed back his chair and got to his feet. A terrible suspicion was stirring in his gut. 'Do you think Rachel knows she's adopted?'

Jacob shrugged. 'Who knows? You'd have to ask your mother. Why? Is it important?'

Matt gave a mirthless laugh. 'It could be.' He raked ba
his hair with fingers that weren't quite steady. 'I slept wi
her.'

Jacob's astonishment was evident. 'You slept with Rachel'

'Yeah.' Matt paced restlessly across the floor. 'I never ev
thought that she might not know about her adoption.'

Jacob frowned. 'But if she didn't know she was adopte
what was she doing sleeping with you? If she thought yo
were her brother...'

Matt shook his head. 'Because she didn't know Sara w
my mother. She thought Sara and I were an item,' he sa
bitterly. 'I knew what she thought and I played upon it.'

'Why?'

'Because I wanted to make her jealous, I guess.' Matt w
impatient. 'Does it matter? The fact is, she had no idea I w
Sara's son. I'm sure of that.'

'You sound very sure of her altogether,' murmured h
father drily. 'Am I to understand that the hangdog expressi
you've worn for the last few weeks isn't just because yo
mother is still staying at Mango Key?'

Matt gazed ruefully at him. 'Yeah, yeah,' he admitted fru
tratedly. 'Call me a fool, if you like, but I've never met a g
like Rachel before.'

Jacob returned his stare. 'It sounds serious.' He pause
'So why haven't you done anything about it before now?'

Matt bent his head. 'I had my reasons.'

'Not wholly commendable ones, by the sound of it,' o
served his father, and when his son didn't answer, he conti
ued, 'What are you going to do?'

Matt blew out a breath. 'I'm going to go and get the tru
out of Sara,' he said, nodding. He made an apologetic gestu
'Sorry about leaving you to it.' He grimaced. 'I've just lo
my appetite.'

'You didn't have much of an appetite to begin with.' Jac

was resigned. 'Yes, go. This is far more important than wasting good steak.'

Matt remembered he'd driven the distance between Jaracoba and Mango Key in record time. And, looking back, he was fairly sure his mother had had some suspicion of why he was home so early even before he'd asked her the burning question.

She'd prevaricated at first, but one look at his grim face had warned her not to lie to him. Using tears as an ally, she'd tried to tell him that losing him as a baby had had a devastating effect on her life. Then, discovering her husband was sterile, she'd only agreed to adoption as a last resort.

'But you never told Rachel you and her father weren't her biological parents?'

'I didn't think it was important,' she'd exclaimed appealingly. 'It wasn't something people talked about in those days. And I don't know why you're getting so chewed up about it now. Rachel means nothing to you.'

'Doesn't she?'

Matt recalled how he'd stared at her until she'd dropped her eyes, and he'd known in that moment that Sara knew exactly what she'd done.

The row that had followed had been brutal. But, dammit, he'd been half afraid—was still half afraid, if he was honest—that his mother had screwed up any chance of his making a life with Rachel. And if that happened he'd never forgive her.

Never.

CHAPTER FIFTEEN

'702.'

Matt said the number to himself as he scanned the keypad situated beside the glass doors. Evidently, with so many occupants, an individual bell system wasn't feasible, and visitors were expected to key in the number of the apartment they wanted.

He was hesitating over whether to select Rachel's number or take a chance on someone else releasing the lock, when a young woman emerged from the building and kindly held the door open for him.

'Thanks,' he said, amazed that the idea of letting a thief into the block didn't occur to her. But maybe she thought he looked harmless enough.

'No problem,' she responded, with an inviting little smile, and Matt realised that she had another agenda entirely. 'Are you looking for someone? Perhaps I can help you.'

Matt's mouth compressed. 'My girlfriend,' he said pleasantly. 'But thanks for the offer.'

The girl's smile disappeared, and with a shrug she walked away. Matt glanced after her and then stifled a smile as he turned towards the lifts. One down and one to go, he thought wryly. If only Rachel would be so accommodating.

He stepped out of the lift onto a rubber-tiled floor. It wasn't luxurious, but it was clean and well-lit, with long windows at each end of the corridor allowing watery sunlight to stream into the hall.

Number 702 was two doors along. And, despite everything that had happened and his own determination to come here, Matt had to admit to a feeling of apprehension.

What if he'd been wrong? He had no real idea what Rachel might be thinking at this moment. Was it possible he'd misunderstood her reasons for leaving?

Dear God, he'd been devastated after that confrontation with his mother. His first impulse had been to get her out of his house, and the very next morning he moved her into the hotel. She'd protested, naturally, but he'd had enough. Then he'd gone to see his father.

As usual, Jacob Brody had been a pillar of strength, and Matt had spent the next twenty-four hours organising his schedule so he could leave the island for a few days. But when he'd gone to the hotel to tell his mother what he was going to do he'd discovered Sara had left the day before.

To say Matt had been angry at the news would have been an understatement. Particularly as it had been too late then for him to get to Montego Bay in time for that evening's flight. Instead, he'd contacted a friend who ran a charter service out of Kingston. He'd flown to London in the luxury of a private jet, mentally chastising himself for not realising his mother would want to get to Rachel first.

There was no bell, so he knocked at the door of number 702. It reminded him of that evening when he'd brought his grandmother's cream to treat Rachel's sunburn. But it also reminded him of what had happened when he'd touched her, and in spite of his nerves his body tightened in response.

There was an eyehole in this door, too, he noticed, and he wondered if Rachel was staring through it right now, trying to decide whether she would speak to him. He had no idea if his mother had been to see her, or what she might have said to her. Sara could easily had lied and claimed he hadn't known

that Rachel was adopted either. Hell, would a mother rea
do something like that to her daughter, adopted or otherwi
He prayed not.

When he heard a key turning in the lock and a chain be
released, he felt a wave of perspiration break out on the b
of his neck. He'd never been so nervous, he realised. G
she'd really messed with his mind.

The door opened a few inches, and he glimpsed the wor
who'd come to mean so much to him hovering just bey
the threshold. She wasn't dressed. Well, not dressed as he
used to seeing her, but he wasn't complaining. The cropped
shirt and what looked like men's boxers displayed a deli
wedge of porcelain skin at her midriff and almost the wh
length of those gorgeous legs.

'Matt,' she said, and he was heartened that she didn't s
the door in his face. 'Wh—What are you doing here?'

'Would you believe, sightseeing?' he asked, trying
humour. But he was honestly weary, and it didn't quite cc
off. 'I guess not.' He grimaced and rested one hand aga
the door frame. 'How about I've come to see you? Does
cover it?'

Rachel's pulse was racing. When she'd heard the knocl
the door she'd been sure it wouldn't be anyone she kn
She didn't expect to see her mother again any time soon,
her father wouldn't call on her at eight o'clock on a Satur
morning.

Living in such a large block, she was used to people get
the wrong apartment, and she'd been quite prepared to igr
it.

Then, when she'd peered through the eyehole, she'd s
Matt and her legs had turned to jelly. Dear heaven, after w
her mother had said she'd doubted she'd ever see him ag

'May I come in?'

He sounded tired, and Rachel immediately stepped to

side to allow him through the doorway. He was wearing a long black cashmere overcoat, open over dark pants and a black tee shirt, and the hem of the coat brushed the lower part of her leg as he went by.

Rachel's breathing was suspended for a moment. And then she gathered herself sufficiently to grab the door and close it again, shutting the much cooler air out in the corridor.

The apartments comprised a small foyer leading into a large living-cum-dining room, with a small kitchen off to the side. But once again Matt's presence made the room seem much smaller, his dark maleness making her intensely aware of her own rumpled appearance.

'I'll just go and put some clothes on,' she began, but he held up a hand when she would have fled into her bedroom.

'No,' he said huskily. 'Don't.'

'But I look—'

'—beautiful the way you are,' Matt assured her, his green eyes shadowed by emotions she couldn't begin to fathom. 'Can we sit down?'

'Before you fall down, you mean?' Rachel knew a surge of anxiety, but she tried not show it. 'You look—exhausted.'

'Gee, thanks. And after I was so complimentary about you,' he remarked wryly.

'You just—well, you don't look as if you've been sleeping very well.' She gestured towards the sofa. 'Go ahead. Sit. I'll get you some coffee.'

'I don't need any coffee.' Matt's hand closed around her bare arm, his fingers dark against the lingering remains of her tan. 'Stay with me. We need to talk.'

'Yes.' Rachel agreed with him there. 'Mostly about what you're doing here.'

'I told you. I'm here because I had to see you.'

Rachel shook her head. 'It's been three weeks, Matt—'

'Do you think I don't know that?'

He spoke harshly, his fingers tightening painfully about

her wrist. Rachel had the feeling he was nearing the end
his tether. The anguish in his face wasn't simulated. He rea
did look worn out.

'Look, let me get you that coffee,' she said, urging him b:
towards the sofa. 'You relax, hmm? It won't take long.'

'I don't want any coffee,' Matt insisted, but to her rel
he did release her arm and slip off his overcoat. He tosse
over the back of the sofa, then sank wearily onto the edge
the cushions. 'There. Will that do?'

Rachel pulled her bottom lip between her teeth. She coul
help but be aware that his eyes were now on a level with
waistband of her shorts. Aware, too, of the revealing strip
midriff it exposed, and the pulse that was hammering in l
throat.

'Okay.' Matt raked agitated fingers over his scalp. 'Fi
of all, has Sara been here?'

Rachel hesitated. 'Ye-es.'

'God, I knew it!' Matt's eyes had darkened again and
exclamation was bitter. 'As soon as she realised what I wo
do, she high-tailed it back here—' He broke off. 'I'm assum
she told you—?'

He sighed, and, realising what he wanted to say, Rac
murmured, 'If you're meaning that I'm adopted, I alrea
knew. I overheard my father and my aunt Laura talking. ?
was of the opinion that I should have been told years ago.

'Thank God for Aunt Laura!' For the first time there v
a trace of humour in Matt's face. 'I bet Sara was livid wl
she found out.'

'Matt…'

'Well…' He was unrepentant. 'When I think of what sh
put me through!'

'What she's put *you* through?'

Rachel looked confused, but Matt only shook his head. '
get to that,' he said unevenly. 'Let me tell you why I did
come to find you before this, right?'

Rachel lifted her shoulders. 'If—if it's important.'

'What the hell is that supposed to mean?' She'd forgotten the precarious state of his emotions. He scowled. 'Of course it's important, dammit. It's the most important thing of all. What do you want to hear? That I can't eat? Can't sleep? That ever since you left I've been blaming myself for ruining your life?'

'Ruining my life?' Rachel stared at him in disbelief.

'Well, okay.' Matt conceded the point. 'Perhaps that was too melodramatic. But, hell, Rachel, you know what I'm getting at.' He paused, and then went on more calmly. 'You were a virgin. You didn't get that way by inviting jerks like me into your bed.'

'Jerks like you?'

'Yeah.' Matt groaned. 'I should have realised how innocent you were. I should have waited until we knew one another better. But—I couldn't keep my hands off you.' He gave a harsh laugh. 'Ironic, isn't it, when I criticised you for not trusting me?'

Rachel frowned now. 'You don't regret what happened?'

'Don't be crazy!'

'Then I don't—'

'I thought that was why you left the island without seeing me again,' Matt interrupted her harshly. He tipped back his head and stared up at the ceiling for a moment, as if he might find inspiration there. 'Do you have any idea how I felt when I arrived back at the hotel and found you'd checked out that morning?'

He looked at her again. 'Obviously not. Well, believe me, I was devastated. And the only reason I could come up with was that you regretted what I'd done and you didn't want to see me again.'

Rachel's jaw dropped. 'But didn't my mother—? Well, no, I suppose she wouldn't.'

'What?' Matt's gaze was intent. 'Tell me that perhaps she

knew why you'd left? Confide that she'd had a cosy little ch
with you? Inform me that you thought I was your brothe
even? Yeah, I think we both know Sara better than that.'

'Oh, Matt!' Giving in to the urge to be nearer to hir
Rachel moved closer. 'And I've been thinking you were gla
you didn't have to see me again.'

'How could you think that?' Matt reached for her then, h
hands closing about the upper part of her thighs, pulling h
between his legs. He leant towards her, pressing his face in
the warm mound of her belly. 'That night we spent togeth
was the best night of my entire life.'

'And—and mine,' whispered Rachel shakily, and Ma
lifted his head to look up at her again.

'So, then, can I take it that you wouldn't have left the isla
if Sara hadn't spoken to you?' he demanded.

'Do you have to ask?' Rachel was trembling now.

'Maybe I just need to hear you say the words,' said Ma
unsteadily, and the sensual quality of his gaze made her kne
go weak.

'I wouldn't have left,' she admitted honestly. 'Not witho
seeing you again anyway.' She felt his thumbs invading tʰ
hem of her shorts and jerked uneasily. 'But you should ha
told me that Sara was your mother.'

'Yeah, I should.' Matt's eyes darkened. 'Though with hin
sight it's probably just as well I didn't, hmm? I mean—Go
can you imagine how you'd have felt if *I'd* told you?'

Rachel let him pull her closer, until her knees were restiʰ
against the junction of his thighs. It was incredibly hard
think with the heat and the scent and the pure male streng
of him surrounding her, so that all she really wanted to ᶜ
was give in to whatever he asked of her.

In an effort to hold on to some semblance of normality, sʰ
said unsteadily, 'You could have told me I was adopted.'

'Oh, yeah.' Matt had to smile at that, his lean face creasiʰ
into the attractive lines she knew so well. 'How would tʰ

conversation have gone, I wonder? Look, sweetheart, Sara's really my biological mother, right? But don't be alarmed because you're adopted, okay?'

Rachel felt a reluctant giggle stir in her throat. 'All the same...'

'All the same—what?' He gazed up at her, his hands slipping inside the hem of her shorts to cup the rounded curve of her bottom. 'Help me out. I'm dying here.'

Rachel quivered. 'Well, you knew I was adopted, and obviously thought I knew it, too. So why didn't you just tell me Sara was your mother?'

'Oh, that...'

'Yes, that.'

He pulled a wry face. 'I didn't deliberately set out to deceive you. But you were obviously looking for your mother, and I knew that as soon as you found her you'd probably leave.' He leant towards her and licked the delicate skin of her midriff. 'And I didn't want that to happen.'

Rachel's fingers lifted to curve around his face. 'Do you mean that?'

Matt uttered a hoarse sound. 'Dammit, of course I mean it,' he said roughly. 'Do you think I like the idea of you thinking I was involved with someone else?'

Rachel shook her head. 'I was so jealous!'

'Jealous?'

'Don't pretend you didn't know.'

'All I know is I've never felt this way before,' muttered Matt a little harshly. With an impatient exclamation, he came to his feet and pulled her fully into his arms.

His mouth found hers almost of its own volition. With one hand behind her head, and the other pressing her close against his aroused body, he took possession of her lips with a heated urgency that betrayed his hungry need. Wedging one leg between hers, he let her feel his erection, drew one of her hands to him so she could shape its pulsing length.

'God, I've needed this,' he muttered at last, his breathing laboured as he sought the sensitive hollow of her throat. 'Just tell me that you feel the same way, or I think I really will go crazy. This has been the longest three weeks of my whole life.'

'And mine,' whispered Rachel, winding her arms about his neck and lifting one leg to stroke her toes down his calf. 'I thought—well, you know what I thought. And finding out Sara was your mother...' She paused. 'Well, I was sure she would convince you to stay away from me.'

'Baby, a herd of wild horses couldn't have kept me away,' he told her fervently. 'As soon as I realised what Sara had told you, I couldn't wait to get on a flight to England.'

Then he was kissing her again, long drugging kisses that weakened her knees and inflamed her blood. The feel of his hard body, the clean male scent of his skin, the possessive touch of his hands, were all sending electric shocks throughout her body. Even the scratch of his night's stubble caused a delicious thrill of awareness to feather her spine.

At last Matt released her mouth again, to say raggedly, 'I want you.' His hands were beneath her tee shirt, and his thumbs were brushing the undersides of her breasts. Then he spread his palms over her nipples and added unsteadily, 'I want you naked, in a bed, with me...'

CHAPTER SIXTEEN

RACHEL's bed was still tumbled, the way she'd left it. The rosebuds on the pillowcases and duvet cover were typically her, and Matt gazed at the bed with a feeling of utter contentment. They were together, and that was the most satisfying thing of all.

It was easy to undress Rachel. Her tee shirt was soon tugged over her head, and the men's boxers were too big for her anyway. Releasing one button had them pooling about her ankles, and Matt took a few seconds just to look at her. This was the woman he'd been searching all his life for, he thought incredulously. And he could hardly believe she was his.

Or she would be, if he had anything to say about it.

His own clothes were less easily discarded. But with Rachel's help he was soon as naked as she was. Then, just for the hell of it, he lifted her into his arms and let her wrap those long legs about his hips.

It meant his erection was close against her bottom, and that was painful. But he could wait, he told himself. They had the rest of their lives together.

'D'you know how much I've wanted to be with you?' he demanded, resting his forehead against hers. He could feel her breasts crushed against his chest, her sweet scent surrounding him. 'I don't think I've had a moment's relaxation since you left.'

Rachel smiled. 'I thought you wanted to go to bed,' she murmured provocatively, and Matt growled deep in his throat.

'I do,' he told her huskily. 'I'm just prolonging the moment. And anticipating what I'm going to do to you.'

'And that would be…?'

'You'll find out,' he assured her, his tone thickening, and, stepping forward, he tumbled her into the bed.

Rachel giggled then, and scrambled away from him. But he crawled onto the bed after her, catching her ankle and turning her onto her back.

'Come here,' he ordered, imprisoning her wrists above her head with one hand. Then he allowed his free hand to stroke a sensuous path from her throat to her breasts and beyond.

She bucked when his fingers slid into her cleft. But she remembered the pleasure he'd given her and spread her legs in innocent provocation.

'Rachel,' he groaned, his arousal not proof against such sensual seduction, and he moved to lie between her legs. Now she could feel his erection pulsing against her stomach, and knew that any control he had was rapidly being eroded.

His mouth covered hers with an urgency that confirmed her suspicions, his tongue thrusting eagerly between her lips. Hot and demanding, it twined with hers, its plunging possession imitating, in so many ways, that other possession he intended to take of her body.

'You're mine,' he muttered, against her mouth. 'And I'm never going to let you go.'

'Promises, prom—' she began, but her teasing words were stifled by his kiss.

Not that she cared. Freeing her hands, she clutched his neck, her fingers tangling in the damp hair at his nape. It was the purest kind of delight to be this close to him again, to know that, whatever happened now, they were together.

He straddled her then, and she levered herself up on her elbows to look down at him. With a confidence she'd hardly known she possessed, she took him into her hand and allowed her fingers to slide along the velvety length of his shaft.

There was a pearl of moisture on its tip, and she knew instinctively what would please him. She used her thumb to remove it and then deliberately put her thumb in her mouth.

That was when Matt lost it. Bearing her back against the pillows, he buried himself in her slick sheath, his laboured breathing an indication of how hard it had been for him to hold back for so long.

'I love you,' he said in a shaken voice, and Rachel's nails dug possessively into his neck.

'I love you, too,' she whispered brokenly, and heard his groan of satisfaction as he buried his face between her breasts.

When he started to move again, Rachel needed no encouragement to move with him. And, although their lovemaking was curtailed when Matt's body convulsed with his release a moment later, Rachel was only seconds behind him.

'I'm sorry,' Matt groaned when he could speak again. 'I've wanted you for such a long time.'

'Me, too,' said Rachel unsteadily, winding her arms around his neck. 'But we have all the time in the world...'

They made love again, and then took a shower together and made love in the shower. Matt's soapy hands made a mockery of any attempt Rachel might have made to resist him, and by the time they tumbled back into bed again they were both exhausted.

They must have slept for a couple of hours, because when Rachel opened her eyes Matt was climbing into bed again, a tray containing two mugs of coffee and a thick ham and cheese bread roll in his hands.

'Hey,' he said, leaning down to kiss her. 'You hungry?'

Rachel dimpled. 'Are you?'

'I'm always hungry—for you,' he appended wryly. 'But we have to satisfy the inner beast as well as the outer one.'

Rachel smiled. 'Are you a beast?'

'You'd better believe it,' he said, setting the tray on his knees. 'I'm your beast, so you'd better get used to it.'

'I can't think of anything I'd like more,' she murmured, wriggling into a sitting position.

She saw Matt looking at her breasts, but this time she made no attempt to cover herself as she reached for one of the mugs. 'Mmm, you're going to love this. Instant coffee!'

'Sweetheart, I'd drink salt water if it would mean I could be here with you,' he said huskily. He paused. 'Did you mean what you said?'

Rachel arched one brow. 'What did I say?' she asked, but she knew exactly what he meant. 'Did you?'

'When I said I loved you?' Matt didn't prevaricate. 'Yeah, I meant it.'

'So did I,' she whispered, her breathing quickening automatically. But when he would have moved the tray aside, she added, 'May I share your sandwich?'

'Is that all you want to share?'

'For now,' she said teasingly. 'Do you realise it's nearly two o'clock?'

'So what? As you say, we've got all the time in the world.' He broke the roll in half and handed it to her. 'I make a pretty good sandwich, though I say it myself.'

'I can vouch for that,' agreed Rachel, after tasting it. 'Among other things.'

'What other things?'

'Matt!' She gave him a reproving look. 'Not now. We have to talk.' She bit her lip. 'I have the feeling my—*your* mother isn't going to be too happy about this.'

'Tough.' Matt was unsympathetic. 'She'll get used to it. What about your father? What will he think?'

Rachel took another bite of the roll. She chewed for a moment and then she said, 'I don't think he'll mind at all. He's only ever wanted my happiness.'

'I think I'm going to like him.'

'I hope you do.' Rachel took a sip of her coffee. 'I just hope he and Mum can resolve their differences.'

'Well, that's their affair.' Matt pulled a face as he tried his coffee, but he didn't put it down. 'I guess it was hard for your father when Sara insisted on keeping in touch with me.'

'Yes.' Rachel nodded. 'Particularly as he suspected your father still cared about her.'

'Oh, God!' Matt laughed now. 'Well, I can certainly reassure him on that score. No one regretted the incident with Sara more than Jacob. Oh, don't get me wrong. He never hesitated when it came to taking responsibility for what had happened. And when I was born he'd have moved heaven and earth to gain custody of his son—me. The fact that Sara didn't want to keep the baby made everything so much simpler.'

'So how did you feel when Sara started visiting you?'

'Honestly?' Matt grimaced. 'Weird.' He paused. 'I met her in New York the first time. She'd found out I was going to Princeton, and I guess she regarded that as neutral ground.' He shook his head. 'But, man, although I knew Diana wasn't my mother, she'd always been there. Sara was a stranger to me. And when she started criticising my father I didn't like that much either.'

'You must have got quite shock when she turned up on St Antoine.'

'You'd better believe it.' Matt put his coffee on the bedside table and relaxed back on his elbows. 'I'd honestly never thought she'd come there. She knew how Jacob felt about her. It was really bad taste, particularly as he'd been ill and wasn't really equipped to deal with her.'

'She stayed with you, didn't she?'

'Yeah.' Matt gave Rachel a rueful grin. 'I mean, I didn't want her there, but she couldn't stay at Jaracoba, and I didn't particularly want her talking about our relationship at the hotel.'

'So tell me about your house,' said Rachel, deciding they'd

said enough about Sara for the time being. 'Is it on the ocean, as—as my mother said?'

'Mmm.' Matt nodded. 'But you'll see it soon enough.'

'Will I?'

'I hope so.' He was solemn now. 'I want you to come back with me.'

'To St Antoine?'

'Well, it's going to be your home,' said Matt reasonably. 'I have no intention of leaving you here for Sara to corrupt you again.'

Rachel finished her coffee and put it back on the tray. 'She didn't actually corrupt me,' she ventured, but Matt was having none of it.

'She let you think you'd been having a relationship with your own brother,' he retorted grimly, turning to imprison her beneath him. 'I think that qualifies.'

Rachel lifted a hand to stroke back the tousled hair from his forehead. 'I'm so glad you're not my brother.'

Matt groaned. 'Don't even think about it.'

'But I don't know if I can come back with you,' she said reluctantly. 'I have a job. Responsibilities.'

'I'll find you a job on St Antoine.' Matt grinned. 'You can help my father write his memoir.'

'Oh, Matt…'

'Do you want to come?'

'Need you ask?'

'Okay. Just leave it to me, then. After what I've been through these last few weeks, handling your boss will be child's play.'

Rachel sighed. 'You make it sound so easy.'

'It *is* easy.' Matt pushed himself up onto his knees. 'Now, there's only one other thing I need to ask you…'

EPILOGUE

THEY were married at the small church in St Antoine three months later.

Matt would have had the ceremony the week after they returned to the island. But Diana, who was organising the event, said she needed more time to ensure that Rachel had a day to remember.

'And me?' Matt had said, and Diana had given him a playful smile.

'I think all your days are going to be days to remember from now on,' she said lightly. 'Now, go and tell your father his lunch is ready.'

Rachel loved Matt's house as soon as she saw it. Unlike Jaracoba, it was a sprawling beach bungalow, with over a dozen reception rooms and half a dozen bedrooms besides. There was a fully equipped gym, and a pool, and it was only yards from Mango Cove, where Matt had taken her on her first morning on the island.

'I wanted to show you my house then,' he confessed. 'But, apart from the fact that Sara was there, you didn't exactly encourage me to pursue a relationship.'

'And did you want to?'

'Oh, yeah.' Matt was very definite about that. 'I knew I wanted you the moment I saw you. But I've already told you that. Stop fishing.'

'And I didn't know it, but I wanted you, too,' admitted Rachel shyly. 'What a fool I was.'

'Well, you're my fool now,' teased Matt, earning a playful slap. 'And I love you, little fool. For ever and a day.'

The wedding was a huge success. Rachel wore a cream moiré gown, with an overskirt and train of pearl-studded silk. She carried a bouquet of roses and baby's breath, with Matt's engagement ring—an exquisite diamond solitaire—her only jewellery.

Matt, in a black tuxedo, looked big and dark and handsome, and when he placed his wedding ring on her finger Rachel was the envy of every woman present.

Rachel's parents attended the wedding. They stayed at the hotel, and, although they were not exactly reconciled, they were not exactly estranged either. Aunt Laura was there, to give the happy couple her endorsement, and all in all Rachel thought the day was everything she could have wished for.

She and Matt spent an idyllic honeymoon in Italy, and then returned home in time for the hurricane season.

'I told you not all days were lovely on St Antoine,' Matt said one morning, waking to find his wife seated on the windowseat of their bedroom, watching torrential rain falling past the windows.

'Uh, no, that was Amalie,' retorted Rachel, smiling as her husband got out of bed and came to join her. 'But, anyway, I don't mind the rain. So long as it doesn't last too long.'

'It won't.' Matt seated himself behind her and drew her back into his embrace. He was naked, and she felt his morning erection nudging her bottom. 'How are you feeling?'

'Better since I threw up,' she admitted ruefully. 'Did I wake you?'

'No,' he lied, but she knew he was aware of every aspect of her pregnancy.

He'd already expressed the opinion that they should have waited, that he didn't want to share her with anyone else.

But Rachel knew what he was really worried about was the fact that her biological mother had died just after giving her birth.

'I'll be fine, you know,' she murmured, tipping her head back against his shoulder. Her hands curved over the slight swell of her stomach. 'Besides, I want your baby. I want to feel it growing inside me. To know that he or she is the ultimate proof of how much I love you.'

'I know.'

Matt bent to caress her shoulder with his lips. He wasn't convinced, and she knew it, but she also knew he'd do anything to make her happy—and if that meant lying about his own fears so be it.

In fact, their child was born just six months later, in the bedroom they used when they stayed at Jaracoba. Matt had wanted Rachel to have the baby in the hospital in town, but the doctor had agreed that in the circumstances there was no reason why she shouldn't have the baby where she chose. And having Jacob and Diana around was definitely a bonus.

In consequence, Matt was the first to hold their son when he came, kicking and screaming, into the world.

'A lusty infant,' declared the doctor admiringly, and Rachel, who had insisted on having the baby by natural means, gave him a tired but triumphant smile.

'Like his father,' she said softly, earning a look that promised retribution later from her husband.

'He's beautiful,' she said, when Matt came to lay their child in her arms. 'Isn't he?'

'Like his mother,' agreed Matt, perching on the bed beside her. He bent to kiss her flushed face. 'Did I tell you I love you?'

'Not for the past couple of hours,' she murmured, feeling his arm slipping around her. 'Hmm, shall we call him Jacob, after your father?'

'Jake,' said Matt, shortening it. 'Yeah. Jake Brody. I like it.'

Jacob Brody was thrilled to hear they were going to call the baby after him. He and Diana would make perfect grandparents, and even Sara and Ralph appeared at the baby's christening.

'Do you think we brought those two together again?' asked Matt, as he and Rachel strolled on the beach at Mango Cove after the celebrations were over.

'Well, they brought us together,' murmured Rachel softly. 'And that's the most important thing, don't you think?'

And Matt agreed.

* * * * *

CLASSIC

Harlequin *Presents*

You can find more information on upcoming Harlequin®
titles, free excerpts and more at www.Harlequin.com.

HPCNM0512

REQUEST YOUR FREE BOOKS!

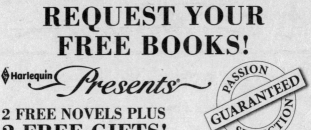

2 FREE NOVELS PLUS
2 FREE GIFTS!

YES! Please send me 2 FREE Harlequin Presents® novels and my 2 FREE gifts (gifts are worth about \$10). After receiving them, if I don't wish to receive any more books, I can return the shipping statement marked "cancel." If I don't cancel, I will receive 6 brand-new novels every month and be billed just \$4.30 per book in the U.S. or \$4.99 per book in Canada. That's a saving of at least 14% off the cover price! It's quite a bargain! Shipping and handling is just 50¢ per book in the U.S. and 75¢ per book in Canada.* I understand that accepting the 2 free books and gifts places me under no obligation to buy anything. I can always return a shipment and cancel at any time. Even if I never buy another book, the two free books and gifts are mine to keep forever.

106/306 HDN FERQ

Name _____ (PLEASE PRINT)

Address _____ Apt. #

City _____ State/Prov. _____ Zip/Postal Code

Signature (if under 18, a parent or guardian must sign)

Mail to the **Reader Service:**
IN U.S.A.: P.O. Box 1867, Buffalo, NY 14240-1867
IN CANADA: P.O. Box 609, Fort Erie, Ontario L2A 5X3

Not valid for current subscribers to Harlequin Presents books.

**Are you a current subscriber to Harlequin Presents books
and want to receive the larger-print edition?
Call 1-800-873-8635 or visit www.ReaderService.com.**

* Terms and prices subject to change without notice. Prices do not include applicable taxes. Sales tax applicable in N.Y. Canadian residents will be charged applicable taxes. Offer not valid in Quebec. This offer is limited to one order per household. All orders subject to credit approval. Credit or debit balances in a customer's account(s) may be offset by any other outstanding balance owed by or to the customer. Please allow 4 to 6 weeks for delivery. Offer available while quantities last.

Your Privacy—The Reader Service is committed to protecting your privacy. Our Privacy Policy is available online at www.ReaderService.com or upon request from the Reader Service.

We make a portion of our mailing list available to reputable third parties that offer products we believe may interest you. If you prefer that we not exchange your name with third parties, or if you wish to clarify or modify your communication preferences, please visit us at www.ReaderService.com/consumerchoice or write to us at Reader Service Preference Service, P.O. Box 9062, Buffalo, NY 14269. Include your complete name and address.

Harlequin *Presents*

Live like royalty…if only for a day.

Discover a passionate duet from

Jane Porter

When blue blood runs hot…

When Hannah Smith agrees to switch places for a day with
Princess Emmeline, a woman who looks exactly like her, she
soon ends up in some royal hot water. Especially when Emmeline
disappears and Hannah finds herself with a country to run and
a gorgeous, off-limits king she's quickly falling for—Emmeline's
fiancé! What's a fake princess to do?

NOT FIT FOR A KING?
Available June 2012

And coming soon in July
HIS MAJESTY'S MISTAKE

Available wherever books are sold.

www.Harlequin.com

HP22130

The legacy of the powerful
Sicilian Ferrara dynasty continues in
THE FORBIDDEN FERRARA
by USA TODAY *bestselling author Sarah Morgan.*

Enjoy this sneak peek!

A Ferrara would never sit down at a Baracchi table for fear of being poisoned.

Fia had no idea why Santo was here. He didn't know.

He *couldn't* know.

"*Buona sera,* Fia."

A deep male voice came from the doorway, and she turned. The crazy thing was, she didn't know his voice. But she knew his eyes and they were looking at her now—two dark pools of dangerous black. They gleamed bright with intelligence and hard with ruthless purpose. They were the eyes of a man who thrived in a cutthroat business environment. A man who knew what he wanted and wasn't afraid to go after it. They were the same eyes that had glittered into hers in the darkness three years before as they'd ripped each other's clothes and slaked a fierce hunger.

He was exactly the same. Still the same "born to rule" Ferrara self-confidence; the same innate sophistication, polished until it shone bright as the paintwork of his Lamborghini.

She wanted him to go to hell and stay there.

He was her biggest mistake.

And judging from the cold, cynical glint in his eye, he considered her to be his.

"Well, this is a surprise. The Ferrara brothers don't usually step down from their ivory tower to mingle with us mortals. Checking out the competition?" She adopted her

EXP0612

most businesslike tone, while all the time her anxiety was rising and the questions were pounding through her head.

Did he know?

Had he found out?

A faint smile touched his mouth and the movement distracted her. There was an almost deadly beauty in the sensual curve of those lips. Everything about the man was dark and sexual, as if he'd been designed for the express purpose of drawing women to their doom. If rumor were correct, he did that with appalling frequency.

Fia wasn't fooled by his apparently relaxed pose or his deceptively mild tone.

Santo Ferrara was the most dangerous man she'd ever met.

Will Santo discover Fia's secret?

Find out in THE FORBIDDEN FERRARA by USA TODAY bestselling author Sarah Morgan, available this June from Harlequin Presents®!

Copyright © 2012 by Sarah Morgan